"So how about it? Will you be my hero?"

Ross's resolve almost crumbled as he found himself wanting to be her hero in more ways than one. But their plans were incompatible. He shook his head, clearing it. "I'm sorry."

She didn't flinch, budge or blink. "You know, I'm not going to leave you alone. You'll have no peace until you give in and do the show."

He didn't doubt her for one minute. She'd already shown she didn't give up easily. "I really hate to tell you this, but it won't do any good." He wasn't going to tell her how close she was getting. But almost as though she could see it in his eyes, she smiled and stepped out of his way.

"We'll see about that, cowboy. I haven't given up on Hollywood and I'm not giving up on you. You can count on that."

Books by Debra Clopton

Love Inspired

*The Trouble with Lacy Brown #318
*And Baby Makes Five #346
*No Place Like Home #365
*Dream a Little Dream #386
*Meeting Her Match #402
*Operation: Married by Christmas #418
*Next Door Daddy #428
*Her Baby Dreams #440
*The Cowboy Takes a Bride #454

*Mule Hollow

DEBRA CLOPTON

was a 2004 Golden Heart finalist in the inspirational category, a 2006 Inspirational Readers Choice Award winner, a 2007 Golden Quill award winner and a finalist for the 2007 American Christian Fiction Writers Book of the Year Award. She praises the Lord each time someone votes for one of her books, and takes it as an affirmation that she is exactly where God wants her to be.

Debra is a hopeless romantic and loves to create stories with lively heroines and the strong heroes who fall in love with them. But most importantly she loves showing her characters living their faith, seeking God's will in their lives one day at a time. Her goal is to give her readers an entertaining story that will make them smile, hopefully laugh and always feel God's goodness as they read her books. She has found the perfect home for her stories writing for Love Inspired and still has to pinch herself just to see if she really is awake and living her dream.

When she isn't writing she enjoys taking road trips, reading and spending time with her two sons, Chase and Kris. She loves hearing from readers and can be reached through her Web site www.debraclopton.com, or P.O. Box 1125, Madisonville, TX 77864.

The Cowboy
Takes a Bride
Debra Clopton

Steeple
Hill®

Published by Steeple Hill Books™

STEEPLE HILL BOOKS

Steeple
Hill®

ISBN-13: 978-0-373-87490-3
ISBN-10:   0-373-87490-1

THE COWBOY TAKES A BRIDE

Faith is being sure of what we hope for and certain of what we do not see.
—*Hebrews* 11:1

To my sister Cindy Drabek and my brother Ricky Patrick. I love you and am blessed to have you both in my life. God bless you and your families!

Acknowledgments

I'd especially like to acknowledge the contributions of the following people:

Senior editor Krista Stroever, because her advice never fails to help take my books to the next level.

A special thank-you to editorial assistant Elizabeth Mazer. Her line edits were wonderful and this book is so much better because of them!

Thanks to executive editor Joan Golan for what she does for Steeple Hill, overall. What a blessing she is to so many and especially to me.

And a big thank-you to editor Louise Rozett for her work on this project. Louise and Elizabeth both made me feel like I was in great hands while my editor was out of the office.

Chapter One

Ross Denton yanked his gloves off and glared at the tractor. Between beavers trying to turn good grazing pasture into a lake, and a new tractor that was out to win the lemon of the year award, his usually cheerful mood had taken a swift dive south. Striding to his truck, he headed toward town, determined to accomplish something productive with his day.

Once he hit the blacktop, the two short miles into Mule Hollow flew by, and within minutes he'd parked at the end of Main Street and was stalking toward Pete's Feed and Seed. If Pete could order in what Ross needed for his tractor, and get it overnighted, then maybe tomorrow would be a better day.

Instantly his attention was snagged down the sidewalk by a blonde in a black ruffled shirt, *zebra*-print pants and a pair of strappy sandals with heels as tall as fence posts! She was wrestling with a suitcase stuck in an ancient station wagon—not exactly a customary sight in a small Texas town such as Mule Hollow.

With his hand on the feed-store door, Ross paused and watched the woman fighting with the case. The ugly vehicle looked like the one his mother had driven when he was about ten. Faded green, with signature wood panels running along the sides, it had seen better days. But he wasn't looking at the car as much as the woman. She had her back to him, and as he watched she stuck one ridiculously high heel against the fender, clasped the handle of the suitcase and pulled.

"Whoa," Ross yelled, charging toward her when the bag popped free and she stumbled back. Too far away to save her from landing on the plank sidewalk, he cringed when she hit the rough wood with a thud. *Ouch.* That had to hurt.

The fact that the suitcase had landed on top of her, then rolled off, couldn't have felt good, either. She seemed to be crying when he got there. Hunched over, shoulders shaking, she sobbed into her hands.

He crouched beside her. "Ma'am, where does it hurt?" He placed his palm on her shoulder, not knowing how to console her, but knowing he had to try.

She took a shuddering breath and looked up at him with bright eyes the color of green olives and gold swirled together. He'd never seen hazel eyes with quite that intensity—or so full of laughter!

She was laughing. The sound finally registered as she gazed at him, grinning widely. She had the cutest dimples.

"Too funny." She waved her hand in front of her face and bit her lips, but giggles came out anyway.

"You're not hurt?" he asked, embarrassed that he was grinning with her. She could be hurting despite her laughter. People reacted strangely to pain sometimes.

She nodded. "I'm fine." Her features relaxed a bit as she took a slow breath. Her dimples didn't completely disappear, leaving her with a mischievous look. He wondered if that was a true reflection of what lay beneath that lively persona.

"Sugar, what in the world happened?"

Ross looked up to find Haley Wells, Mule Hollow's only real-estate agent, standing in the doorway of her office. "She took a tumble and now she can't seem to stop chuckling," he said.

"That's Sugar. When she gets tickled, she can't stop laughing sometimes," Haley declared. A phone inside the office started ringing. "Busy day! Help her, Ross, I've got to get that call. Boy, am I glad you're here to help me, Sugar!"

"Sure thing," Ross replied. He'd already planned to help her up. He was more than aware that he liked what he saw when he looked at her. Though he wasn't fond of the zebra-striped pants and the skyscraper heels, he did like those dimples. The woman's face was open and inviting, with a girl-next-door appeal that hooked him. And there was something extraordinary in the way her eyes captured the light.

"Thanks, cowboy." She took his offered hand with a firm grasp and smiled as she rose to her feet.

"Ross Denton, glad to be of service." Still holding her hand, Ross felt a kick of pure attraction that sent his pulse humming.

"Sugar Rae Lenox. I used to be Haley's assistant in L.A." She tugged her hand free and waved toward the building. "I'm here to help run her office for a short while."

He noted the "short while" with disappointment. "Nice to meet you, Sugar Rae. You must get asked this all the time, but are you named after Sugar Ray Leonard?"

She nodded. "It's a long story, though, and I have to get moved in here, so I won't bore you with it right now. Thanks for picking me up off the ground." She turned back to the vehicle and grabbed hold of another suitcase. The way she'd packed the back end of her station wagon rivaled the dam-building techniques of his pesky beavers.

"Here, let me get that for you." He reached out for the handle.

"No need, I can get this one. I packed it."

"Looks like you used a bulldozer."

"How did you guess?"

He eyed the conglomeration of suitcases, boxes and housewares stuffed inside the car. "Just lucky. But really, I'll help you unload that. Here." He carefully tugged the suitcase out and then a few boxes, setting them on the sidewalk between them.

Sugar shrugged. "Suit yourself, cowboy. I'm certainly not going to turn down two strong arms. But I'm going to warn you one last time. If you know what's good for you, you'll turn and run far, far away. Unpacking my stuff is going to be a challenge you might regret getting involved with."

"Sugar," he drawled, grinning into her playful eyes. "I do believe I'm up for the challenge."

She arched an eyebrow. "Oh yeah, cowboy? We'll just have to see about that, won't we?"

She was teasing, but he wasn't. Looking at her, he knew he meant it.

Only minutes ago he'd thought this was going to be a dismal day.

Wrong. The day's potential had just skyrocketed, and gauging by the twinkle in her eyes, the days to come in Mule Hollow promised to be anything but dull.

The lyrics of "I Need a Hero" were playing inside Sugar's head as she and the ever-so-dashing Ross the cowboy grinned at each other.

Who was this gorgeous guy? *Okay, back it up, sister!* She was not here to flirt, date or otherwise entangle her personal life in this tiny town. She wasn't here because she actually wanted to be…oh no, this city gal wanted to be back in L.A. starring in the fantastic romantic comedy in which she'd almost scored the leading role. The one that, like all the others, she'd just *barely* missed out on. She didn't have time for real-life romance—she was here because her dreams were going down the tubes and she was desperate to make something happen. Age mattered in Hollywood, and if she wanted to be America's next sweetheart then she had to give her acting career a shot in the arm before she was considered over the hill! Mule Hollow was that shot. She was here to get a play going, a summer stock that would get some buzz happening. Then she'd be back to L.A., where she could finally snag some much-needed attention from those directors who kept passing her over.

So there, she told herself firmly. She wasn't here to gawk at gorgeous cowboys with striking green eyes and sexy voices. But still… The thing was she *did* need a hero for the show she was going to produce, and if this walking, talking, long tall Texan wanted the job, he had it. On the spot.

"I'm back," Haley said, bursting through the open doorway and interrupting Sugar's runaway thoughts. "Grab a bag, everyone, and let's get the apartment unlocked before the phone rings again," she added in a rush. "Lately there are more and more people calling and wanting to look at property out here. You just wouldn't believe how Molly's articles have attracted people to this area."

"That's great to hear," Sugar said. Molly was a journalist who lived in Mule Hollow and wrote a syndicated column about life there—the town that had advertised for women to come and marry all their lonesome cowboys. The column was unbelievably popular, and Sugar was counting on that popularity to help her make her dreams come true. This was going to work. It *had* to. And looking at the handsome cowboy beside her helped keep her thinking positive.

Haley grabbed one of the cases "Ross the hoss" had set on the sidewalk while Sugar had been drooling over him, and headed toward the side of the building.

Sugar grabbed the box at her feet as Ross slipped the strap of her travel bag over his arm, then picked up her two larger suitcases. His cowboy hat dipped as he motioned for her to go ahead of him. Nerves jangling, she led the way around the corner to where Haley was already climbing the stairs up the side of the building.

"I came in earlier and turned on the air for you," Haley said as she pushed open the door at the top of the stairs.

Sugar followed her. The blast of coolness was a welcome feeling from the end-of-June heat. Inside, she stopped short. "Oh. How cute!"

"No lie." Ross peeked in over her shoulder, effectively distracting Sugar with his closeness. The man smelled *good.*

"I bet it never looked this nice before," he stated, his breath whispering across her cheek.

Sugar inhaled slowly, turning her head toward him. Their faces were not even three inches apart. "It's lovely," she said, clearly not talking about the apartment. His beautiful green eyes darkened with interest. Instantly, her mouth went dry.

"I couldn't agree more," he said, lowering his voice to a raspy rumble. "Do you mind?"

"Mind?" she asked. "Mind what?"

"Moving over so I can come in?"

Almost choking with embarrassment, she fled across the room, giving him all the space he needed.

What had she been thinking?

The air conditioner was blasting full speed, but there was no air in the room. Zero, nada, zip-o! In fact, the room seemed to shrink like plastic wrap in a microwave as Sugar felt the scorching heat of embarrassment fire up her cheeks. *Really, Sugar, where did your head go?*

"I hope you like it," Haley said. Her back had been

turned and she'd missed Sugar's schoolgirl reaction to Ross. Now she set the case she was carrying down beside the bedroom door and faced Sugar. "Is something wrong?"

"No, not at all. I was just admiring the place." She shot Ross a glare when he smiled knowingly.

Unaware of the tension slicing through the room, Haley rushed on. "I really enjoyed painting it and finding the furniture. I did it with you in mind, because I knew that once it was done, I was going to call you and offer you the job."

Distracted though she was, Sugar was touched. "I love it." She ran her finger over the soft white fabric of the couch.

"Of course, when you add your things, it will come to life. I just tried to find appealing furniture in neutral colors you could work with."

"I couldn't like anything more. Thank you." Sugar hugged Haley, feeling self-conscious knowing that Ross was watching.

"I'll go get some more of your stuff. You two ladies take your time." He tipped his hat and stepped around them, his arm brushing hers as he did.

Sugar knew she was going to love the apartment. But despite her best intentions, it wasn't the place she was thinking about—oh no. It was this cowboy!

Chapter Two

*F*ocus, *Sugar Rae! Focus*—easier said than done, Sugar thought. Ross made her feel like she did just before she walked into an audition: a clash of nerves and adrenaline. It was a very unsettling reaction. Totally unexpected and unwanted.

Trying to pull herself back together, Sugar trailed Haley around the apartment, checking out the bedroom and the small bath. They followed Ross back to the car. To her surprise, other people were waiting to meet her and help unload the car. She was glad for the welcome and for the distraction.

There were the gals from the hair salon across the street, Lacy and Sheri. Sugar knew they were two of the women who'd helped put the tiny town on the map. Ashby and Rose from the dress store were there, too. Sugar felt like she'd already met them since Molly had written about each one in her column. The four ladies from the candy store also took a minute from work to say hi and give her a housewarming gift.

"Wow," she said, gazing at the basketful of mouthwatering chocolates. "To think it wasn't too long ago this town had almost no women. Now look at it." Main Street had filled with women, and they all came together to make a newcomer feel welcome. Sugar was touched by their kindness—and she couldn't wait to dig into her basket! She felt a little guilty that she wasn't completely happy about being there.

Haley sighed. "There was a time when I thought there was no hope for this place. Boy, was I wrong," she said, smiling. "I know you're here to help me out and to boost your acting career, but I think the town will grow on you, too."

Sugar gave her a playful but serious look of warning. "Maybe, but Haley, I *am* leaving."

They all started filing up the stairs, each carrying something from the car. Sheri gave Sugar a wide, sassy grin as her fancy red boots clicked on the steps. "Have you met the posse yet?"

"The posse?"

Lacy called up from behind her, "That's what Sheri calls Norma Sue, Esther Mae and Adela. The ladies who came up with this great plan to save their town. You'll love them."

Sugar glanced over her shoulder at Lacy. She was talking about the matchmakers! The ladies were the stars of Molly's column. Her curiosity piqued by why Sheri called them the posse. Distracted, she barely noticed when the large box of kitchen supplies slipped a little from her grip as she reached the top of the stairs. Ross was coming out the door, taking one look at her load and reaching for it.

"I'll take that," he said. "You should leave the heavy stuff for me. Remember, I told you I was up for the challenge." He took hold of the box, but Sugar didn't release her grasp. She looked up at him with teasing skepticism, trying to cover her attraction. "I don't know, you look a little shifty, like maybe you might skip out early on me."

He hoisted the box into his arms as if it was a tiny matchbox. "Not a chance, sweetheart."

She grunted and reached behind him to hold the door for him. It wasn't enough that the man had a slow, easy drawl that sent her insides into a riot. He had to be chivalrous, too. And he had a nice sense of humor…. She caught Lacy and Haley looking up at her, and checked her thoughts when she saw the smiles they were sporting. When she followed Ross inside, Sheri was smiling the same smile.

"*Gorgeous,*" Sugar mouthed silently, behind his back, then headed down the stairs again to get another box. Of course, thinking he was good-looking was where it stopped for her. Jittery nerves and an overactive imagination be hanged, she hadn't come here to date. Her goal was going to take every spare minute and ounce of focus she had, if she was going to accomplish it.

Sugar wasn't really worried about Haley and her new friends getting ideas. They'd learn soon enough that she was very single-minded when it came to making it as an actress. It was the dream she'd had since childhood. The dream that had helped her make it through difficult days as a little girl too sick to play outside with her friends. Too sick to *have* friends... It was a dream she knew was supposed to come true, and she would not give it up.

Emptying the station wagon took no time at all with everyone helping. They'd all gone back downstairs and were standing around talking, but once Ross saw that there were no more boxes or suitcases to carry, he tipped his hat and started to leave.

He'd only taken a step before turning back. "I'm in the book. If you need anything else, just give me a holler. And if you just happen to come up with any other challenges you want to issue, I'm only a phone call away." His words held a cockiness and teasing. His eyes, however, were completely sincere.

Sugar watched him head down the street and disappear inside the feed store. Only then did she fully relax. His departure was a relief. Despite her determination not to let herself be interested in him, she'd kept getting distracted every time those green eyes of his met hers. The man had a way of gazing at her that made her feel she was the only person around. It was a little unnerving. She wondered if every woman he looked at felt that way. That might come in handy when she talked him into trying out for her show. Those piercing eyes would be able to connect with an audience, one-on-one.

"It is really great to have you here," Lacy said, dragging Sugar's head out of the clouds. "It's just totally exciting! When Haley announced you were an actress and wanted to start a theater in town, I got goose bumps. I really did. We do plays periodically and I'm seeing good things in here—" she tapped her temple "—with you at center of our productions. I can't wait to get together and toss ideas around."

Not knowing how much Haley had explained or even how much Haley understood about her plans, Sugar just said, "That'd be great."

Just then, a car pulled into a slot across the street in front of the salon. "That's my three-o'clock cut," Lacy said. "But we'll talk soon. I do love people with big ideas, especially ones that are going to help Mule Hollow grow. Catch you later." She spun and jogged off to greet her customer.

Sheri started to follow her, but paused. "Hey, are you looking for a husband?"

"Not at the moment. Why?" Sugar wasn't sure what to make of Sheri.

"If that's so, then when you meet the posse, you might want to hide those sparks flying between you and Ross. That is, unless you're prepared for a little help in the romance department." She widened her eyes in an exaggerated look of warning.

"Hey, the guy is drop-dead gorgeous, and I'm not blind. But aside from the fact that I'm totally focused on my career, I'm *not* here to stay. Surely once the matchmakers know that, then sparks or no sparks, they'll not get any ideas."

Sheri sent her a wry glance. "None of that will matter, believe me. Ross Denton isn't just a pretty face. Oh, no.

He's a true-blue, all-around great guy. He's ready to settle down and believe me, if they see the way he's gawking at you—well, I've got two words for you. Look. Out." She turned, then strode down the stairs.

Sheri implied this could be trouble. Sugar watched her until she disappeared into the salon. Naaa. Good luck to any matchmakers who thought they could hook her up without her consent. If they saw her as a target, they were going to find they might as well be shooting blanks when it came to Cupid's arrow.

Not that she wasn't going to be looking…eventually. Down the road, around the bend a few times, over the hill and through the dale, whatever in the world that meant. But it wasn't going to happen anytime soon.

An hour later, Sugar entered Sam's Diner escorted by Haley and the infamous matchmaking posse. They were a bunch of really delightful ladies—sort of Miss Bea meets Lucy and the Golden Girls. She was enjoying her chat with them as she walked into the place when suddenly she looked around and the reality of her situation set in with blunt clarity. She was a city girl. She loved being a city girl, and took the things that entailed for granted. She was talking about *coffee*. Not just any coffee, but sweet, creamy mocha and cinnamon, caramel. She *loved* her Starbucks, and if she'd had any ideas about her favorite latte while in Mule Hollow—well, that misconception melted the instant she walked into Sam's. She screeched to a halt, and the heavy wooden door almost hit her in the backside as it swung shut behind her. She was so shook up, she hardly noticed. Old wood tables, plank floors and weathered wood walls greeted her. No sir, she wasn't getting a caramel-mocha latte with a sprinkle of cinnamon here, that was for certain. A craving for her favorite drink grabbed hold of her and she bit back a groan, realizing she'd be lucky if Sam offered skim milk with her coffee. For certain she'd have to kiss whipped cream goodbye. By the looks of this place he might even cook his coffee out back over a campfire!

Oh dear, it really felt as if she'd stepped back in time, and for a girl who loved the modern-day conveniences associated with the city, "back in time" didn't sound so good.

"What do you think?" Haley asked, eyeing her curiously.

"Wow. It's…it's very rustic."

Haley nodded. "It is wonderful, isn't it? As long as I can remember, it has always been the same. Sam bought it from the previous owner and didn't change anything, except to put in the jukebox."

Esther Mae Wilcox shot a scowl at the jukebox as fiery as her red hair. "*Much* to our sorrow," she harrumphed.

Norma Sue Jenkins, a robust woman with curly gray hair and a smile that took up her entire face, grinned at her friend. "You know you'd miss it if it died completely."

Esther Mae glared at her. "I'd dance on its grave. If we're going to have to listen to it, the least Sam could do is shake things up a bit. Or you, since you're the one who always works on the thing. Change some songs. Give me some of those new cutie patooties to listen to. Like that sweet little Oakie, oh, what's his name… You know, he sings about the beach and he married that darling little movie star Renée Zil-something-or-other."

Sugar chuckled. "Renée Zellweger and Kenny Chesney."

Esther Mae's eyes lit up. "Yeah, that's who I'm talking about." She shook her head. "I exercise to his sweet voice in the mornings on my mini trampoline."

Sugar got a visual, which wasn't hard, since Esther Mae had on a cantaloupe-colored jogging suit with big red strawberries splashed everywhere.

When she and Norma Sue continued their animated discussion about the jukebox, Sugar realized this was an ongoing debate. They were a hoot. Life wasn't going to be boring with them around.

Adela, seemingly oblivious to her friends' argument, slipped into a nearby booth and patted the seat beside her. Sugar kept her eyes and ears on the floor show as she sat down.

Their movements brought Esther Mae up short, and she shook her red head. "Sorry, we tend to lock horns about that jukebox, but don't pay us any mind." She slid into the seat across from Sugar, and Norma Sue did the same. "We're more interested in hearing all about you. Everything."

Adela smiled. Sugar knew from the papers that she was Sam's wife, and the one who'd originally come up with this unusual way to save her dying town. She was a doll, with electric-blue eyes made brighter by the pixie-cut, snow-white hair that perfectly framed her face. She was elegant and serene, and a complete contrast to her friends. Not that she was shy; Sugar didn't get that impression at all. Just composed, and unruffled.

She patted Sugar's arm with a delicate hand. "Don't look so worried, dear, we're not going to give you the third degree," she said, a gentle smile creasing her face. "Are we, girls?"

Norma Sue and Esther Mae didn't look to be in total agreement on that, but they nodded.

Haley had pulled up a chair at the end of the booth, but didn't seem interested in adding to the conversation. She was clearly content just watching them. Her eyes twinkled and Sugar studied her with interest. The real-estate office where they'd worked before had been very stressful. With so many properties to be handled, and with so much money at stake, that was to be expected. Sugar knew it had been one of the factors that sent Haley running back to Mule Hollow. She'd told Sugar the people there were good, genuine folks who cared about each other like they were family. Then there were those newspaper articles by Molly. They, too, painted the town in a positive light.

Sugar hadn't really believed them. Haley and Molly lived here and loved it, so Sugar had figured their information was probably a little biased. It had to be.

Still, as she let her gaze roam around the table and thought about the other women who'd welcomed her, she suddenly wasn't so sure whether there was a bias or not.

Could Mule Hollow really be as nice as it seemed?

She was still pondering that when Sam came out of the back. A spry man with a brisk, bowlegged gait, he looked as if he might have been a jockey in his younger days. He held out his hand right away. "How do."

Sugar slipped hers into his and almost flinched. What a strong grip! "How. Do. *You.* Do," she managed to reply.

Grinning, he released her hand and rammed his fists on his apron-covered hips. "What can I bring ya?"

How about an ice pack? she wanted to say, but ordered a glass of ice water with lemon instead. Everyone else ordered tea and coffee.

"So, give us the scoop. Haley here already told us you're an aspiring actress," Norma Sue said.

"Technically, she already is an actress," Haley clarified.

"In anything we would know?" Esther Mae leaned forward on one elbow. "I just love the movies."

Sugar hesitated, thinking of all the films she'd almost had a recognizable part in. Or the ones she'd had a decent part in, only to have her scenes end up on the cutting-room floor. God had put this dream in her heart, but it hadn't been easily attainable. "Well, I've actually done more commercials than movies you might recognize. I did a Folgers commercial and—"

Esther Mae slapped the table and her eyes went wide. "You did an *insurance* commercial—the one where the gal fell out of the hot-air balloon! That was you, wasn't it?"

Here it went. "Yes, ma'am, it was me."

The redhead slapped the table again. "I knew it. That was a funny commercial. Why, the way you sort of flipped and dived out of that basket…" She was overcome with chuckles, and began to wave her hand in front of her face as she tried to get ahold of herself. "I still nearly split a gut, thinking about the way you looked. Your face was stretched back by the wind, sort of flapping—"

"That was you?" Norma Sue shrieked.

Sugar nodded. She hated that insurance commercial. Hated knowing that was all anyone knew her from. That after all of her hard work, it was her most memorable moment. At least in the coffee commercial she'd done some real acting, and not just physical comedy. It was depressing. But that was going to change. It was. And besides, actors got their start in commercials—even stupid commercials—every day.

"I've seen that ad. You were funny," Adela said, as Sam returned with a tray of drinks.

"So tell us about your plans," Norma Sue urged. "Haley said you want to start an actual acting troupe. A theater of some sort."

"Yes." Sugar sat up, energy surging through her just from thinking about it. "I want to do a summer stock–type production. I think it would be great to have both acting and singing in it. Have you ever been to Branson, Missouri? I'm thinking more along the lines of a play, but those shows inspire me to think some singing cowboys would be great. Haley told me about the wonderful community center you have, and I thought it would be the perfect place to start a show. I want something that runs week after week. One that could draw attention to the town and to me. I need some great reviews that Hollywood will pay attention to. You know, so I can get that breakout part I so desperately need in order to succeed."

Norma Sue looked thoughtful.

"You came to the right spot. We have some *very* talented cowboys in our town!" Esther Mae exclaimed. "Bob Jacobs, Molly's husband, sounds like Tim McGraw. He's just fabulous. And there's more, too."

Norma Sue and Adela shot a look at each other. "Is something bothering you?" Sugar asked.

"We have some folks here who don't want anything to do with getting on stage," Norma stated. "We leave them alone."

Okay, Sugar thought, wondering about the odd statement. Suddenly, Haley set her tea down, drawing all eyes to her. "I just realized we might have a problem. This show would run every weekend, right?"

Sugar nodded. "To get a buzz going that could draw some major attention, I need to do at least three shows a weekend. If I could get it together by the first week of August and carry it on through October or maybe November, that would be a good run."

Norma Sue frowned. "This *is* a problem."

"Oh, dear," Esther Mae said. "It certainly is."

Okay, they'd successfully put a fireball in the pit of her stomach. Sugar looked at Haley, then back at the ladies, waiting for someone to tell her what this problem was.

"You see, dear—" Adela looked at her kindly "—our

community center is used for much more than just plays. We have wedding receptions there and various other town activities. For instance, Pete's Feed and Seed hosted a one-day seminar there last Saturday for all the ranchers. One of the big feed companies was introducing a new grain or something. So if we have your show going on there every weekend, it would displace all the activities we might otherwise schedule."

Talk about a kink in a good plan. "I hadn't thought about that." Sugar's mind whirled as she contemplated this obstacle. "I *should* have, though. I just got so carried away with the idea," she groaned.

"Now, now, don't give up." Esther Mae turned serious. "There has to be a way."

Think, Sugar. Think. "A barn!" she exclaimed, instantly pushing the gloom back into the shadows. "They called summer stock 'strawhat' because most of them were performed in adapted barns. So all I need is a barn. And *then* some cowboys."

The table erupted with rapid-fire exclamations of relief and agreement. Discussion ensued about what attributes this barn should have. Everyone agreed it needed to be big and close to town. And most important, it couldn't be one that the owner was using.

"Plus the rent would have to be dirt cheap," Sugar added. She had to be frugal. "At least until we see how it takes off." She was going for broke, praying that God was going to work this out for her. She was stepping out in faith, trusting that this was where she was supposed to be. "Better yet maybe I could talk the owner into some kind of partnership."

Norma Sue frowned. "There aren't that many barns close to town. The only one I can think of not being used is Ross Denton's. And that's not good."

Esther Mae's smile faded. "It sure isn't."

"Why not? If he's not using it, then what's the problem?" Despite their frowns, Sugar felt providence kicking in again. It had to be, because Ross was the only cowboy she'd met so far and just look how he was working into her plan. That couldn't be a coincidence. It was amazing, actually. But even Haley appeared hesitant. "What?"

"Ross doesn't want anything to do with entertainment," Esther Mae said.

"And we let him be."

More than a little confused, Sugar glanced at Norma Sue. "I don't understand. He seemed more than pleasant today when I met him." She thought about the cowboy's flirting. "Besides, he told me that if there was anything he could do for me, to just call."

The ladies didn't seem convinced.

"Haley, what's up?" Sugar asked.

"I really don't know everything. He didn't live here when I was a child. I'd actually forgotten all about his ties to Branson."

"Ties to Branson!" Sugar exclaimed. "This is just getting better and better." Why, if he had ties to Branson, he might be able to help her with more than just letting her use his barn.

"But he came here because he was burned out from being in the spotlight," Adela said, immediately getting Sugar's attention. "His family on his mother's side still has a successful show there. Ross was part of that. But you see, he gave it all up six years ago and came here to the ranch his father's family left him."

Norma Sue nodded. "He came here wanting nothing to do with singing or performing. All that boy wants to do is ranch, and find a good woman to build a quiet life with here in Mule Hollow. We've respected his wishes all these years."

"That's right," Esther Mae interjected. "We feel kind of protective of him."

Despite what they were saying, Sugar's adrenaline had started pumping. Two weeks ago, she'd received a rejection for a role in a movie that her agent had thought she was a shoo-in for. It had been the worst day of her life. All the optimism that kept her going had gone up in smoke. The horrible self-defeating voice in the back of her head that she'd been trying to ignore had started up again telling her to lay her dreams down. Lay them down? How could she? And then Haley had called and asked her to take a break and come out to Mule Hollow. At that very moment Sugar had been drowning her sorrows in a bucket of ice cream and watching Paul Newman's story on the Biography Channel. He'd got noticed by Hollywood while he was in a summer-stock production. Inspiration had hit, and Sugar realized that the tiny Texas town might be just the place God was leading her to go. That it wasn't God's voice in her head telling her to forget her dreams. And now here she was, with even more proof that providence had led her here. She smiled from her heart. "Ladies, don't worry about anything. Just tell me where this perfect barn is and I'll take care of the rest."

First thing tomorrow, she'd go out there and see the place. Then she'd give Ross Denton a call. Yes, indeed, things were looking good.

Chapter Three

The sun hadn't come up yet when Ross walked toward Sam's Diner the morning after meeting Sugar Rae Lenox. He glanced at the second-story apartment a couple of doors down and wondered if the sliver of light he could see through the curtain meant she was awake. He liked her. Pure and simple. He couldn't remember the last time anyone had caught his interest so completely, and he wasn't planning to waste any time before getting to know her better.

Of course, it was too early to go knocking on her door, so he headed on into Sam's for breakfast. Unsurprisingly, he wasn't the first customer. Applegate Thornton and Stanley Orr were, as usual, Sam's first clients of the morning. The two old men were already deep into their morning checkers match. Haley was Applegate's grand-daughter, and Ross didn't think there had ever been a prouder grandpop. He wondered if App knew Sugar.

"Mornin', fellas," he said, heading toward the counter.

"What's good about it?" Applegate grunted, staring at the board.

"Don't pay no mind to him," Stanley told Ross. "He jest has a burr in his saddle this mornin'. 'Cause he's plain loco." The last few words were said louder, obviously as a footnote to some conversation they'd been having before Ross walked in.

Both men usually spoke louder than needed, since they both wore hearing aids. There was an ongoing debate among the local cowboys whether either of them really needed a hearing aid, or whether they were using them as an excuse to talk loud whenever they wanted, and listen in on everyone else's conversations by pretending they couldn't hear. That lack of hearing sure seemed convenient at times.

Applegate frowned, his thin face drooping into its perpetual cascade of wrinkles. "I'm tellin' ya it works. I saw this woman on one of them late shows last night, and she was tellin' all kinds of stuff about body language. It made good sense."

"It's all crazy," Stanley grunted. "You can't tell me you know just from watchin' a man pull up his socks that he's smitten with a gal."

"This here highfalutin' woman said it was true. That and some other stuff." Applegate looked up as Ross sat down at the counter. "Ross, like I done told Stanley and Sam, this body-language expert said that if a man is talkin' to a woman and he reaches down to pull up his socks—well, that right thar is a sure 'nuff sign that he's smitten."

"Ross," Stanley said, pausing to spit a sunflower husk into the spittoon. "You ever reach fer yor socks when you was talkin' to a female? *I* never did."

Ross wasn't too sure he wanted to be in the middle of this conversation. "Well, no sir, not that I can remember."

Stanley nodded. "See thar? Hogwash. That's what that is."

Applegate scowled and turned red. "You had to see it. That woman made it all sound perfectly legitimate."

Ross couldn't imagine he'd ever feel the need to pull up his socks while talking to a woman, not even yesterday, when he'd been talking to Sugar Rae Lenox. And if ever there was someone who had him "sure 'nuff smitten," she more than fit the bill.

Sam came out of the back, snagged a cup and set it down in front of Ross. "Mornin' to ya, Ross."

"Mornin', Sam."

"Those beavers still chawin' down your trees and damming up your creek?"

Ross shook his head in disgust. "They can cut down trees faster than a logging crew. I'm heading back out there in a few minutes and I'm afraid to see what else they've done. Not only that, I had tractor trouble again yesterday and I didn't get my hay cut."

"That ain't no good."

"No sir, it sure isn't."

The door swung open and Clint Matlock walked in, followed by a handful of other wranglers. Sam snagged five mugs, one on each finger, slapping the first down on the counter as the rancher took a seat beside Ross.

"How's it going, Clint?" Sam asked, filling the cup.

He yawned. "Late night. Thanks for this, Sam. I already drank half a pot at home. But nothing has a kick like your coffee."

"That's my special blend. I stick my ornery finger in the water before I brew it." Sam arched a bushy brow and grinned, then headed around the counter toward the booth of cowboys.

Clint chuckled and took a slow swallow and looked sideways at Ross. "Hear you helped our newest resident move in yesterday. Thought I'd warn you that Lacy came home very inspired by the way you were looking at Haley's new office manager."

"I didn't make any pretense of hiding my interest."

"That so?"

Ross took a drink of his coffee. "Mmm-hmm. I've got to go check on those worrisome beavers that are trying to turn my pasture into a lake, then I'm coming back to town to stake my claim on that one."

His friend gave him a speculative look. "That sounds promising. You need any help?"

Ross grinned. "I think I can handle asking a girl out on a date all by myself. But thanks for the support, buddy."

Clint shook his head. "I meant do you need any help with the beavers? I'll let you do your own romancing. Whether Lacy and the other women of Mule Hollow let you alone is a whole other ball game."

Ross wasn't worried. "I don't plan to give them enough time to get an organized matchmaking plan in order. I'm sure once they see I'm already matching myself up, they'll sit back and let me alone. They've never tried to fix me up before."

Clint cupped his coffee and breathed in the aroma, looking at Ross over the brim. "They only leave couples alone when they don't really see anything special between them. If, however, they see lasting possibilities they will watch carefully and tweak as necessary."

"Did you just say 'tweak'?"

Clint grimaced. "'Fraid so. Obviously, up to this point, my friend, you haven't had 'tweak potential.' But Lacy saw something yesterday, and all that may be about to change."

"Hey," Stanley called, looking up from his checkers. "Maybe she saw him reach fer his socks! App here thinks that'd be the way to knowin' who's smitten and who ain't."

Applegate scowled. "I'm tellin' ya that woman last night on Leno made sense. She had more degrees tagged onto the end of her name than Liz Taylor's got ex-husbands, so she should know."

Stanley jumped two of his checkers and grinned impishly, making Ross wonder if he was picking on App to distract him from the game.

"Don't ask," Ross said, shaking his head when Clint looked at him. "App watched something on TV about body language, and he figures he's got it all figured out."

"So did you reach for your socks?" Clint asked with a chuckle.

"Might as well have, from what we heard," App said.

"You two need to take your act on the road," Ross teased.

"You think yor family would take us on?" Stanley asked.

"Are you kidding? They'd snap you two up in a minute. Y'all could give ole Homer Lee a run for his money."

Applegate grunted. "I'm bored stiff sittin' here lookin' at Stanley every day, but you couldn't pay me enough ta git up on a performin' stage."

Ross took a drink of his coffee, remembering all the years he'd spent on stage. "I couldn't agree more. I just thought I'd offer. A good comedic act can always find an audience."

Stanley spat a sunflower husk into the spittoon. "I'd pay good money fer App ta stay off the stage."

That got a laugh from everyone.

Sam topped off Ross's and Clint's coffee. "Do you ever miss it, Ross?"

"Nope." He took a drink, feeling the burn. "Twenty years in the spotlight was more than enough for me. But I could still put in a good word for you two if you want me to," he said, laying money on the counter and standing. It was time to go to work.

"We might be bored," Applegate said, "but wild horses couldn't get us ta leave Mule Hollow."

Ross grabbed his hat and snugged it down on his head. "You've got that right. This is the place to be."

And it was. He was happy with his life.

He'd started performing on stage at age four, singing with his grandpop. It hadn't taken long for him to be listed on the marquee as a box-office draw. Even for a little kid, seeing his name up on that sign had been a thrill. He'd been twenty-four when he'd realized he couldn't do it anymore.

Didn't want to do it anymore.

His grandpop had been dead for a couple of years, and living his life around two shows a day, six days a week, had started to give Ross ulcers. Living someone else's dream would do that to a body.

After stepping out on the sidewalk, he strode toward his truck and climbed in. This was his dream. Overseeing the land, the legacy he'd inherited from his dad's family. Running cattle, building up his ranch, even with broken tractors and irritating beavers included. God had blessed him with great family on both sides of the tree. He'd had a choice of two separate ways of life, but this was the one he wanted to cultivate. This was the one he wanted to raise his kids in.

Backing the truck out, he glanced up toward the apartment where Sugar Rae Lenox now resided. He was living his dream, but he was ready for the good Lord to send him a soul mate. Truth was, he'd had his name up in lights, but the only place he wanted to see it these days was on a wedding certificate.

He just had to find the right woman to sign on with him.

Sugar couldn't wait to see the barn.

She knew she should ask beforehand, but she couldn't help herself. The ladies had said it was on the outskirts of town, and she had to view it. Had to know if this would be a place where she might be able to set up her show.

The very idea of putting on a strawhat production of

some sort in a real barn excited her more than even the thought of having it in the community center. An honest-to-goodness barn theater added an entirely new element to the project, making her excitement level jump to unforeseen heights.

"Thank you, Lord," she gasped when she saw the big old barn come into view. The thing was huge. And ancient. And lovely. Simply lovely. For a gal who'd been doubting herself, her dream, her faith, this felt like a sign that God was still on her side. So far everything about coming to Mule Hollow was proving to her that the voice of doubt she'd begun to hear was unfounded. God wasn't the one whispering in her ear, telling her to abandon her dreams.

Smiling, she studied the building. The rambling place drew her as she yanked the car to the side of the road and switched off the ignition. Feeling as giddy as a child, she scrambled out and hurried across the cattle guard. She was so engrossed in getting a closer look that the fact she was trespassing didn't cross her mind as she walked down the rutted dirt road. Okay, so it did flit through her head for a second, but she didn't give it any serious consideration. Ross didn't look to be the kind of guy who would mind, and besides, she was on a mission.

It was a looming two-story structure with a pitched metal roof. The boards were weathered, the red paint faded to a charming patina that gave it character, like wrinkles on a face. The double doors at the front were at least twelve feet high, if not fifteen. They were also slightly ajar. Sugar hadn't come this far to stop now. Couldn't even if she'd felt like it. She slipped inside. And stopped.

As a kid with a weak heart, relegated to a life of sitting on a couch, or in bed between hospital visits and surgeries, she'd become a dreamer out of necessity. She'd lived because of her dreams, because of her optimistic outlook. God had given her life, but he'd sustained her with her dreams. Standing inside the door of Ross Denton's old barn, she knew this was where those dreams were at long last going to flourish.

If there was such a thing as love at first sight, Sugar had found it. There was a huge space inside. Stalls off to one side stood below a loft that ran across the first third of the building, leaving the rest of the barn open all the way to the rafters. Morning sunlight filtered through windows, letting in a soft glow and making Sugar feel as if she was actually walking into her dream.

Heart pounding, she moved to the center of the barn floor, turning an old five-gallon bucket upside down to sit on. Totally in awe, she placed her elbow on her knee and her chin on her fist as her mind flew free, filling with ideas. This was it. This was the place. No longer was this just a dream.

Oh no, this was a full-fledged done deal. She could picture it all. People laughing, kids clapping.

Reviewers raving… Oh yeah, this was perfect. And Ross Denton was the key to it all. He was the guy that was going to help her make her dream come true.

The last thing Ross expected to see as he drove out from the back pasture was Sugar Rae disappearing inside his barn. For a minute he thought he'd imagined her, but the sight of her unmistakable vehicle by the road proved that his imagination wasn't playing tricks on him.

Shutting off his truck, he crossed the pasture, more than a little curious to find out what Mule Hollow's newest resident was up to. Maybe her car had broken down? But why would she be driving around out here at nine o'clock, when her apartment was right above her office, and she'd come to Mule Hollow to work?

At the doors, he peeked inside. She was sitting on a bucket in the center of the barn, obviously lost in thought.

Today, she was dressed in a gauzy yellow dress that draped over her like a tent, with a pink shirt underneath that matched her pink canvas shoes. The outfit was a far cry from the heels and zebra pants of the day before, but still just as interesting. She wasn't boring, that was for sure.

Wondering what she was thinking, he stepped inside. "Please tell me you missed me already and you came out here looking for me," he teased.

She shot to her feet with a shriek. "Where did you come from?"

Not the reaction he'd hoped for. "Whoa there, take it easy. I didn't mean to startle you. I was coming out of the pasture through the woods and saw you entering the barn."

She blew out a gusty breath. "You wouldn't have surprised me if I hadn't been so lost in my thoughts. I love your barn. Do you have any idea how wonderful it is? I mean, can you imagine all the history that happened in here? The square dances and maybe church socials…"

"I like it. There is a lot of history to this place," he agreed. She was a bundle of surprises. "I didn't take you as a history buff, though."

"Actually, I'm not. I just felt this overwhelming connection when I walked in. It makes what I have to propose to you all the more important."

He smiled at her dramatics and was all ears. "Propose away. You have my full attention."

Her eyes widened more, if that were possible. "You see, I haven't come to Mule Hollow just to help Haley. What I really want to do is start up a summer theater. I'm an actress, and I'm looking to find a way to stand out. I need some good reviews to help me land some better parts. And..." she twirled around, arms out "...this is where I think I can do it. Right here in your barn, Ross Denton. And to make it even more perfect, I hear you have some experience in that department. I just couldn't believe my good fortune when the ladies told me your family has a show out in Branson."

He groaned inwardly as his heart sank. An actress. Of all the rotten luck. "I don't entertain anymore." He sang to his cows sometimes but he wasn't going to tell her that.

She frowned at him, but didn't let it stop her. Her forehead crinkled. "Okay, but I need a theater. And, well, I have a limited budget, so I was hoping, since your barn would absolutely be the perfect place, that I could talk you into letting me work out a deal with you. I want to do something on Friday nights and maybe twice on Saturday, and the ladies said that would take too much time from the community center for me to run the show there. It would knock out too many other things, since I would practically be taking over the place. I completely understand. And it's just fine, since I love your barn. This is the place I'm supposed to be. I can feel it. Have you ever just…" she paused, with the most hopeful expression on her face "…you know, just *known* when something was right?"

She blinked her big eyes expectantly, and his heart sank lower still. Feeling his frown all the way to his toes, he scooped his hat off his head and tried to gather his thoughts. This was not good.

When he didn't say anything, she plunged back in. "I was already thinking of trying something similar to the way they run shows in Branson, so just imagine my excitement when I learned you had experience. But don't worry, I'm thinking smaller." As she rattled on, her voice filled with renewed excitement.

His heart hit rock bottom. "I'm sorry, Sugar, but the answer is no," he said, and before he did something stupid and said yes, he spun on his heel and stalked out of the building.

Chapter Four

"Wait!" Sugar called after Ross, but he just kept on walking. She couldn't believe this. What had happened to the nice Mr. Flirtatious from yesterday? She hurried out of the barn.

"Stop," she demanded as she chased after him. "I don't understand your attitude."

"Look, Sugar," he said, stopping so quickly she almost ran into him. "I never participate in any of the shows they put on here in Mule Hollow because I don't do that anymore. And I don't want it happening on my property. I'm sorry, but the answer is no. And it won't change."

Sugar waved a hand toward the barn. "But it's just sitting there. It doesn't even look like you use it."

"That doesn't matter. You'll have to find another barn. The answer is no."

Watching him walk away, Sugar was almost at a loss for words. Almost. "C'mon, Ross. Give me a break here. I don't know what your problem is, but I'm sure we can work it out. I'm starting auditions pretty soon. I need a place. Work with me here."

He spun, as quick as a gunslinger. She immediately got a visual of him on stage.

His brows creased and she felt a bit of hope, so she smiled encouragingly at him.

"When exactly are you planning on working for Haley?"

"From ten till five, Monday through Friday. The rest of the time is mine to do with what I want. And what I want is to set up an old-fashioned strawhat production."

"Well, good luck finding another place. Really. I mean that. You want a ride to your car?"

"What?" The man couldn't be serious. "*No!* I don't want a ride. I want your barn."

His jaw tensed as their locked gazes held. The air crackled with challenge. And attraction—though Sugar doused *that* quickly enough. The man could help her if he wanted, and instead he was being a pigheaded oaf! What a disappointment he was. She glared at him.

"Look, don't be stubborn. Hop in and I'll drive you. I wouldn't feel right leaving you standing there. I don't want you getting hurt out here on my property."

Now he was back to being Mr. Chivalrous! Sugar took a deep breath and prayed for patience. "I wouldn't want to put you out, cowboy," she snapped, and walked away from him down the rutted path, her dress mushrooming with each stomp of her feet. At the sound of his truck starting, she walked faster, regaining her composure as she went. If he thought she'd given up, he was mistaken.

She just had to figure out the right way to make a comeback…and she would. After all, she was Sugar Rae Lenox. The comeback kid.

He drove up behind her in the big truck, but made no attempt to go around her, and she made no move to get out of his path. He followed her until she walked across the cattle guard, and then paused behind her once she reached her station wagon. Gritting her teeth, she smiled sweetly at him, waved, then climbed behind the wheel and slammed the door.

She noted with satisfaction that Ross wasn't smiling as he drove off.

Good. Maybe his conscience was starting to work on him.

Before she drove back to town, she glanced back at her barn. God was surely smiling on her to have provided such a perfect place for her strawhat production. On that note, she would keep thinking positively. Ross would come around.

He just didn't realize it yet.

"Why didn't you fellas tell me she was an *actress?*" Ross asked the next morning. He was in a foul mood as he sat at the counter at Sam's, nursing a cup of coffee. The disappointment in Sugar's eyes the day before hadn't set well with him. Turning her down—well, really, telling her flat-out *no*—had been his automatic reaction. A gut reaction. And though it was the only answer he wanted to give, he wished he'd said it a better way.

But no was still no, any way you said it.

Especially when it came to him and entertainment. Still, the look on her face had driven him from his bed this morning and to Sam's so early that he'd beaten the old-timers.

"We thought you knew," Applegate said. "Ain't you heard my Haley Bell talk about her friend the actress?"

"No, App, I haven't. I don't have my finger on the pulse of the community like you do," he snapped.

"I didn't think ta tell you," Stanley said as he sat down. He plopped a handful of sunflower seeds in his mouth and started placing his red checkers on the board, ignoring Ross's glare. "Does it bother ya that she's an actress?"

Sam came out of the back and set a plate of pancakes in front of Ross before he had a chance to answer. He liked to eat sweets when he was stressed.

"So does it?" Sam asked.

Ross looked from him back to the checkers players, glad they were the only ones in the diner. "Yes. It does. Frankly, I liked this girl."

"So, what's her bein' an actress got to do with that?" Applegate asked.

"I'm not looking to date a woman just to be dating her. I'm looking for a wife. She's an *actress*. She's got one thing on her mind and that's getting her name up in lights."

"So yer holdin' that aginst her? It ain't like she ain't got a good reason," Applegate grunted.

"That's right," Stanley huffed. "Tell him, App."

Ross's curiosity got the better of him and he set his coffee down. "I'm all ears, App."

"Me, too," Sam said.

"Haley Bell told me that Sugar was a real sick little girl. She was one of them thar preemie preemies or something like that. You know, one of them really tiny premature babies. I thank she weighed about two pounds or somethin'. Can you just imagine that? Anyway, she was a fighter, but it took blame near her whole childhood fer her ta get healthy. She had somethin' wrong with her heart, among other thangs. Had a ton of surgeries and spent a lot of time in front of the television. Said them act'rs helped keep her going." He looked at Ross from beneath caterpillar brows. "No wonder she's got her heart set on bein' one."

The room was silent. Ross sat for a moment and took it all in. Then pushed the untouched pancakes away and stood up to go. He needed to think. "Thanks for telling me that, Applegate. It doesn't change my mind…about anything. Trying to date her or letting her have my barn. But at least I understand her a little better."

As he laid his money on the counter, he could tell by their scowls that they didn't like his answer, but he couldn't help it. Really, it would be better for Sugar if he didn't give in. The woman couldn't understand what she was trying to accomplish.

Putting on a show was a huge undertaking. His grandfather Dupree, or Grandpop, as Ross had called him, started his show "The Singing Duprees" with little more than a guitar, a need to entertain and a steely commitment to give it his all.

Because of that, Grandpop's dream came true, and

he'd lived to see his grandchildren follow him up on the stage he'd built. It had thrilled his soul. Ross could still remember the look of pride in his eyes whenever they sang a song together in front of a packed house.

As a kid all Ross had known was how proud he was to be singing beside his grandfather. As an adult, he'd grown weary of the behind-the-scenes struggles and the exhaustive amount of determination and commitment it took to keep the show going.

Sugar Rae might be looking at a shorter show schedule, but he didn't think she knew what would be required of her to get that curtain up each performance. It was a strenuous, locked-down lifestyle. And it was one he never wanted to experience again.

Ranching was hard work, too. It required long days— sometimes seven days a week. But it was a quiet life, and that suited him.

Clearly, it wouldn't suit Sugar.

He'd talked with her only twice, so realistically, it shouldn't bother him so much that she'd be leaving.

But it did bother him. And she *was* leaving; no doubt about it. She had stars in her eyes and leaving on her mind.

The story Applegate had just told him made him even more certain that the passion he'd heard in her voice was real. He'd come across it many times before during his years on the stage. Plenty of actors with Hollywood on their radar came through Branson looking for experience. It didn't take them long to leave.

He gave Sugar six months, and then she'd be out of

here. He'd do well to keep that in mind, because any time he invested in her would just be wasted time. End of story.

Haley glanced over the top of her computer at Sugar. "Those ads you loaded onto the Web site look great. It is so fantastic to have you helping me. I'm a real klutz when it comes to Web pages and that technical stuff."

"You could learn it. It's just procedure. Once you learn the ropes, you're in."

Haley gave an exaggerated grimace. "Easy for you to say. You know how to do it."

Sugar rolled her eyes and tried to concentrate on work. "If I can do it, you can, and I'm going to teach you while I'm here."

Haley laid her pen down. "I know you don't want me to say this, but I really hope you'll stay on. It would be good for you and for us. You have so much to offer the community."

"You know that won't happen," Sugar said frankly. She needed to nip that idea in the bud pronto. And truth was, if Ross didn't come around, there was no reason for her to stick around. She'd made Haley a promise to come help her get things going with the office, but if she couldn't find a way to help her career, then she was staying in this small town for the absolute shortest time possible.

Haley sighed. "You can't fault a girl for hoping."

Sugar couldn't hold back anymore. "So tell me, what's the story on this Ross guy? He wouldn't even listen to

what I had to say this morning. He seemed different from
the guy I met yesterday—talk about a rude dude. And I
know about rude."

That made Haley laugh, just as Sugar knew it would.
Sugar had been notorious for assisting other assistants in
the office when it came to people behaving badly. "He
didn't know you were an actress. I'm honestly confused
by all of this, too. I really don't know him all that well,
and had completely forgotten about his ties to Branson.
No one ever talks about it anymore. I think his family
comes to visit him some, but they have a really tight
schedule and can't get away that often."

"Still, what's it going to hurt the guy to at least
consider it? Mule-headed, that's what he is. And selfish."

"Will knows him better than I do. Maybe I need to
invite you and him for dinner. We can soften him up.
What do you think? It's worth a try."

Sugar pulled open her top drawer, plucked a green
gumdrop from the bag stored there and bit it in half. She
chewed on one half and squished the other between her
fingers as she thought over her strange encounter with
Ross. "He's going to soften up. I'm going to hound him
until he does. Too much is at stake here. I have to have
his building."

"Are you going to destroy his resistance like you just
destroyed that poor piece of candy?" Haley asked, a smile
in her voice.

Sugar zoned in on the small blob of green goop. "Ack!
Disgusting! What was I thinking?" She shook her hand
over the trash can, but it wouldn't come off. Grabbing a

tissue, she wiped it away. "There. Okay, back to the point. The man will come around."

"How do you know?"

"Because if I have to talk him into it, I will. I'm angry at him right now, but he really does seem like a nice guy. A little moody, but I'm sure that when he sees the show will be good for Mule Hollow, he'll give in. I'm going to calm down and pray about it."

"I'll pray, too. I just can't help thinking God has a plan here." Haley studied her. "This could be very interesting," she said at last. "Ross might not be as wimpy as you think."

"Don't you laugh, the man will surrender. I promise you," Sugar warned, aware of the smile she was trying to control.

Haley held her hand up in surrender. "I believe you. Remember, I've seen you in action. So when are you going to start auditions?"

"I'm going to print up a flyer for Sam's and the feed store, and get things going on Saturday. And since you've taken over booking the community center, I was hoping I could use it for rehearsal. Thanks to my sweet grand-mother I have money stashed away that will finance this venture, if I'm frugal."

"You can use the community center for the auditions and for rehearsal. We'll work something out. I'll also do a sponsorship to help with the cost. After all, this is going to be a great attraction—I really do believe in you, Sugar."

Sugar suddenly felt like crying. "Thank you," she said softly. "That means more to me than you know."

Haley smiled as if it was no big deal, but it was to Sugar. As she was growing up, her parents had seemed to believe in her dream to be an actress, but when it came time for her to head out to L.A., they'd changed their tune. Only then did she find out that they'd supported her dream as a means to help her make it through her illness. They'd thought she'd grow out of it.

She told herself that it didn't matter, but it did. Having someone believe in you was important.

But proving wrong those who *didn't* believe in you could also be great motivation.

It was almost closing time on Saturday afternoon when Ross parked in front of the feed store. He needed to grab some more wire from Pete's, but found himself heading toward the real-estate office instead, despite his determination to stay away. No matter how many times he went over it in his head, he still felt like he owed Sugar some sort of explanation for his abrupt behavior on Wednesday morning.

He wasn't at all sure what kind of welcome to expect as he opened the door and stepped inside.

"Hey, cowboy!"

Her greeting both startled him and made him wary at the same time. "Hey yourself," he said, moving cautiously into the room.

"You're just the man I was hoping would walk through those doors today."

"I am?" He was immediately suspicious.

"Oh yeah. How's my building doing? You know I'm holding auditions tonight?" Her eyes were sparkling.

"I've been monitoring the visitors I've run into over the last couple of days, and I'm feeling more optimistic by the carload. There's been a real eclectic mix of folks. College girls looking for cowboys, weekend browsers shopping at Ashby's dress store, and even older couples just hanging out. I've been polling everyone about why they came to town. Most of them say it's a pleasant day trip. These kinds of people will make a perfect audience when I put my show on in your lovely barn." She was beaming at him when she finally finished.

He wasn't sure whether to be irritated that she hadn't given up on his barn, or amused. "About that—I thought I'd come in here and try to explain myself a little better. There was no excuse for me to turn you down so callously." It was true, he'd concluded. He could have turned her down without being so abrupt.

She waved off his apology. "I'm sure you had your reasons. As I'm also sure that, now you've had time to think it over, you've come to your senses and decided to go into partnership with me on my show." Grinning, she rested her chin on her palm and studied him.

He laughed at her blatant tactics. "You're persistent, I'll give you that."

"Nope. I only want you to give me the use of your barn." She batted her eyes at him. "Just say yes. It's easy."

He was in danger here.

"I promise you," she continued, "people will come out to see my production. We'll do a few skits and some singing, and oh yeah, did I tell you I need a hero? You'd make a great hero."

Man, she really didn't take no for an answer! He liked that about her and found himself wanting to say yes. But that wouldn't be fair to either of them. Still, she was persuasive. What red-blooded American man wouldn't want a woman to think he'd make a great hero? Too bad they were on two different life paths, he reminded himself.

"I'm not your man," he said, hating the disappointment that flickered in her eyes. "Look, I just don't believe you understand what it takes to pull off what you're proposing. There is a lot of work that would have to be done to the barn. It would take time, money, insurance. But most of all, it would take commitment, not just to produce the show, but to keep it running. You're leaving as soon as you get some great reviews. Sorry, but I don't see any commitment in that. I know that sounds harsh, but it's the truth. That's what I came to say." He tipped his hat and headed toward the door, needing to leave before he weakened. He wasn't expecting her to shoot out of her chair and jump between him and the door.

"You can't say no." She placed her hand on his chest, stopping him. "Don't you get it? I *need* your barn. It's the only place that will work."

The panic in her words matched that on her face, making Ross falter. Those pleading eyes twisted his gut more than he was prepared for. A picture flashed through his mind of a frail little girl sitting in front of the TV. "I'm sorry, but that's just the way it is," he reiterated, feeling like a bottom-feeder for denying her this. He hung his head, trying to keep from giving in, and found himself looking at her feet. She had *smiley faces* on her big toenails, almost hidden by the flip-flops with large, frilly tassels that swamped her tiny feet.

The smiley faces were as unexpected as she was.

"What size shoe do you wear?" His own blurted question startled him more than the smiley faces, and he swung his head up. Now he felt like a bottom-feeder *and* an idiot.

The panic from seconds before vanished as she chuckled, sticking her foot beside his size twelve without missing a beat. "A five narrow. A bit of a difference?" She wiggled her smiley faces at him. "Your foot is just the right size for a hero, don't you think?"

She looked up at him and flashed a smile complete with dimples. This was crazy! Crazy for certain, but he lost his breath looking at her.

"So how about it? Will you be my hero and *pul-leese* let me use the barn?"

His resolve almost crumbled as he found himself wanting to be her hero in more ways than one. But their plans were incompatible. He shook his head, clearing it. "I'm sorry."

She didn't flinch, budge or blink. "You know I'm not going to leave you alone. You'll have no peace until you give in and at least agree to rent me the building. My feet might be small, but my determination is huge."

He didn't doubt her for one minute. She'd already shown she didn't give up easily. He knew he needed to get out quick before he gave in, but curiosity got the better of him. "So why aren't you some big movie star by now? With your winning ways, I figured you'd camp out on a director's front steps and talk him into putting you into his movie."

"My agent won't let me," she huffed. "Says it wouldn't do me any good."

"I really hate to tell you this, but it won't do any good with me, either." He wasn't going to tell her how close she was getting. But almost as if she could see it in his eyes, she smiled and stepped out of his way.

"We'll see about that, cowboy. I haven't given up on Hollywood and I'm not giving up on you. This is fair warning."

Ross grinned in spite of himself. "Fair enough." It wouldn't do her any good, but he enjoyed her spirit, despite his own reservations.

Having closed for the day, Pete was driving off as Ross walked out onto the sidewalk, with Sugar on his heels. So much for accomplishing what he'd come to town for.

"Tryouts start at seven tonight."

"I hope you have a good turnout. But I have a feeling you're going to see what I've been trying to tell you. You don't know what you're getting into, Sugar."

"You could help me and fix all that."

He hesitated before opening his truck door. "That's what I've been trying to explain without being too harsh. I don't want to. Have a nice day, Sugar Rae."

Hands clasped behind her back, she rocked forward on her size-five feet and locked determined eyes on him. "I plan to, Ross Denton. You can count on that."

Live and learn, Ross thought as he drove away. It

was obvious the woman would do what she was going to do regardless of what anyone advised. So be it. He shouldn't feel guilty for not helping her. But truth was, he did.

Chapter Five

"So when is the show scheduled?" a cowboy named Trace asked from the second row.

Sugar was pleased with the turnout. Glancing around the roomful of cowboys, she felt sure that the talent she needed was here. Except, of course, Ross was conspicuously absent.

"I was hoping to open in five weeks. We'll have to work really hard initially, but then the rehearsals can just be once or twice a week. Since we'll only be doing a Friday-night show and two shows on Saturday, we won't need to run through the whole thing every night." Sugar was ready to continue by telling them about the different songs, and asking if any of them played musical instruments, when she noticed the frowns rippling around the room. Several of the cowboys began talking to each other, and shaking their heads.

Head shaking was never a good thing.

"Is something wrong?"

"Well, yes ma'am, there is," a cowboy drawled, standing up and hooking his thumb in a belt loop. "We didn't realize you were looking for a long-term commitment. We're *cowboys*. We have work to do."

Another one stood, joining the mutiny. "We just can't make a commitment like that. Our hours are long and unpredictable. We can take off for the occasional show, like we've done in the past. But every Friday night and two times on Saturday, plus practice—well, that puts most of us out."

A whiplash of dread slammed into Sugar. "But think about all the benefits."

"What benefits?"

What benefits? "The experience and the exposure." Once she'd said the words out loud and looked around the room, the "benefits" suddenly didn't sound logical to her ears. The cowboys' blank looks told her exactly how out of touch she was with what they were looking for in life. It wasn't a career in the spotlight…. As a matter of fact, gazing at them, she felt foolish. Sugar was used to living in a town where everyone was looking for a way to break out. Clearly, in this room, she was the only one with that goal.

"I was afraid of this," Lacy said, worry in her eyes.

"We thought you were going to rehearse a few times, then do a show and be done with it. Like Lacy always does," yet another cowboy said as he stood up. By now, they were popping up like weeds.

Not good. Not good at all. Sugar could feel their withdrawal, knew they were about to make a break for the door.

"But it'll be fun. Surely you can find the time—"

"I'm real sorry, but I can't commit to something like this," Trace the cowboy said, stepping toward the door.

Other apologies rolled across the room, and within moments, just as she'd feared, the full room began to empty.

Sugar watched as, one by one and two by two, every man in the room respectfully tipped his hat at her, then headed out the door.

The icy grip of panic tightened around her throat with each one. She was so distressed, she couldn't speak and had to fight to keep from throwing herself in front of them. It was one thing to embarrass herself before Ross by letting down her guard, but she couldn't let an entire room of men see her lose it.

"Don't get discouraged," Esther Mae said after the last booted, spur-clinking male disappeared out the door. "There has to be a way around this."

"That's right," Adela said. "God will show the way if this is what He wants."

Sugar didn't like the sound of that. *Lay down your dream*—the words came back to her and she struggled to ignore them. It was getting harder and harder to stay positive on this roller coaster.

"I think He is," Lacy said. "There's a way around this. You may just have to come up with an alternate plan."

"Seems like that's the ongoing theme since I arrived," Sugar murmured, unable to hide the discouragement she was feeling as she slumped into a chair. "If I can't get a barn or cowboys, then I'm doomed."

"Now, now, it'll work out," Esther Mae soothed. "I know it will. After all, you're going to be the main attraction. Right?"

"That's absolutely right," Norma Sue answered for her. "First off, you will get the barn. Second, all you have to do is put a show together where you're the star. Then simply build some entertainment around you that can be easily changed, show to show. You'd just have to alter the approach, and get the fellas to commit to short rotations."

"That's a great idea," Lacy exclaimed. "The guys really do enjoy doing the shows. The girls all get a kick out of seeing them sing, and most local cowboys are up for whatever will help them find the right gal."

"I don't know." After this latest disappointment, Sugar was reluctant to get her hopes back up. "They all sounded pretty firm about it being too much to commit to. And Ross hasn't budged on the barn."

Lacy sat down beside her. "Don't let this get you down. You trust the Lord, right?"

Sugar was *trying* to trust the Lord. "That's why I'm here. I believed this is where God wants me to be. I'd so hoped this was where my dreams were going to get their start."

"Then keep that chin up," Esther Mae said, with all the enthusiasm of a coach.

Sugar laughed. "Okay, okay. I'm not giving up."

"That-a-girl," Norma Sue said as the others chimed in. "Mule Hollow is *not* a place where people give up."

"You know what?" Sugar said as realization dawned.

"Ross knew. He realized the guys would react this way. He tried to warn me, but I didn't get that until now."

Adela spoke up. "He does have experience. Not just in the entertainment business, but in the cowboy business, too."

Sugar narrowed her eyes. "He stood right there in front of me and watched me be happy and positive, all the while knowing the cowboys were going to turn me down flat."

Indignation pushed her up from her chair. "Of all the downright dirty, mean tricks," she said through gritted teeth, while everyone looked at her with startled expressions. They could probably see steam boiling out of her ears. "If you will excuse me, I believe it's time for me and a certain cowboy to have a little heart-to-heart."

She strode down the aisle and out the door. She could hear everyone scrambling out of their chairs, and then clambering out to the plank sidewalk. But she didn't look back as she crossed the street. Her mind was focused on Ross Denton.

He thought she was a pushover. He thought that she was just some happy-go-lucky balloon head who hadn't thought out any of this! He could have warned her, *really* warned her. Actually said the words. Even if he didn't want to let her use his barn, or take a part in her production, it wouldn't have hurt him to give her a little advice!

"Sugar," Lacy called, stopping her as she was about to close the door of her car. "Maybe you need to calm down just a little."

"Calm down? I don't think so. Thanks for showing up,

girls, but I have urgent business to attend to now. I have a cowboy to lynch."

She slammed the door and cranked the ignition, glancing out the window before backing up. The older ladies flanked Lacy, and they watched as she turned her car toward Ross's place.

It was only then that she remembered that while the old barn was on a part of his ranch, she had no idea where his house was located. Stomping on the brake, she rolled down her window. "Could one of you please tell me where he lives?" From the looks that shot between them, she was afraid they wouldn't.

But Norma Sue, bless her heart, propped her hands on her hips and grinned. "After you pass the lane that takes you to the barn, there will be a big curve about a mile down the road. His is the first drive on the left."

"It's a good piece down the lane," Esther Mae added. She was smiling, too. "Don't kill him," she giggled, and everyone grinned. It was quite strange, actually.

Sugar didn't know what in the world they found funny about this. That mean, horrible man had basically made a fool out of her. In a huff, she pressed on the gas.

It was time for a showdown.

With the crickets providing backup, Ross lay beneath his tractor, singing while he worked. It was a George Strait number about a father's love, an old song Ross had sung with Grandpop in the early days. That was appropriate, since today was his dad's birthday. Earlier, he'd called Jud Denton and wished him a good day. Before saying goodbye, they'd talked about the tractor Ross was ready to burn, the beavers he was ready to shoot and finally the woman he couldn't get out of his head.

The one he continued to feel guilty about.

He was well aware of the time. Sugar was probably in the middle of her tryouts. And more than likely, things weren't going well.

He'd been trying not to think about it, he couldn't help himself. After all, it was Sugar, the woman who'd imprinted herself on his mind like a brand. They'd talked three times in the five days since she'd moved to town, and he couldn't get her out of his thoughts.

Since he'd turned twenty-seven and began heading toward thirty, he'd started to see areas of his life where he was changing. Like this intense tunnel vision he'd developed over finding a wife. He'd heard it called nesting, which made him feel a bit like Elmer Fudd for some reason, or the Pillsbury Doughboy.

Still, he was feeling the need to marry...and although he knew Sugar would be shaking the dust of Mule Hollow off her cute little feet before the New Year set in, she had captured his attention like no other woman ever had. This was not a good thing.

"I thought you were a nice guy!"

Sugar! At the sound of her angry voice, he jerked up and slammed his head into the undercarriage.

"Ohhh! Are you all right?" she gasped, all the anger dissipating with the thud of his head against steel.

"I'm fine," he grunted, pulling himself from beneath

the tractor as he rubbed his forehead, squinting at her through one eye as pain radiated from the knot he could feel forming above his other eye.

"You have a lump," she cried, dropping to kneel beside him. She touched his forehead with tentative fingers.

"It'll go away," he said, still squinting at her. The pain evaporated the second her fingers touched him, or maybe it was the instant she leaned close and he caught the scent of her—like spring, soft and fresh. For a brief moment, they just stared at each other. Then she blinked, her eyes hardened and her fingers fell away.

"Serves you right," she said. "You *knew* those cowboys would walk out on me the minute I told them what the show would require."

"Yes, I did." Ross stood up and grabbed a rag off the tractor's fender, wiping his hands clean. "Like I told you before, this isn't Hollywood, where everybody works a job around their auditions. This is *cattle* country. The cows come first. That's what cowboys do—they tend their animals. And that means they work as long as the day's duties require, and into the night when needed. You should have realized coming into it that acting wouldn't be paramount on their list. That you didn't only proves that you have no idea what you're trying to undertake. Especially since your production depends on having a local cast and crew."

She crossed her arms, looking as if she'd like to give him another lump on his forehead. But he knew she couldn't deny the truth.

"That may be true, but you still could have warned me.

No, wait. I know. You didn't tell me because you can't be bothered with anything that has to do with putting on a *show*. That is such a cop-out."

"Maybe I should have told you. I didn't think you would listen, but that's irrelevant. The point is that this is just the beginning of things to come that you haven't a clue about. Acting in a commercial and pulling off a production are two entirely different animals. I've been trying to make you understand that. You don't have what it's going to take."

She glared. "You don't know me. You don't know anything about me! You say I don't have what it takes, but let's talk about you! You are a Singing Dupree. A *Dupree,* for goodness sakes! You're telling me I don't have what it takes, and yet you gave up on your dreams to come here? To do this?" She waved a hand toward his tractor. Her meaning was clear.

"For starters, I didn't give up on my dream. I'm *living* my dream. But you wouldn't understand that—"

"No, I wouldn't! I don't get a guy with a God-given talent throwing it away. But what I really don't get is being selfish. Don't you see what this production could do for the town? Just think of the economics involved. Don't you realize that we could make a difference by helping draw more people here on the weekends? Think of the revenue that would bring into the community."

He'd been struggling to remain calm, given what he'd learned about her past, but this statement snapped his patience. "C'mon, Sugar. Admit it. You don't care about this community. You're here to get what you can, and then move on. You want to stand there and judge me, then look me in the eye and tell me I'm wrong."

At least she seemed embarrassed by the truth. She glanced away momentarily. "Okay, it's true that I'm not staying. But that doesn't mean I don't care. Though I've only been here for a short while I already feel a connection to these wonderful people."

"Maybe so, but you could pull out of the whole deal at a moment's notice."

"No. I wouldn't do that."

"If Hollywood called right in the middle of a show and offered you a nice, fat role, you cannot stand here and honestly tell me you wouldn't drop us and run back there without so much as a backward glance." He clenched his jaw to keep from saying more.

Her eyes glittered as she stared at him. "I've worked my *heart* out to try and make it in Hollywood," she said at last, her voice low. "I have studied. Paid my dues. Been so close to getting my break that—" She stopped, her voice breaking on the last word.

Oh man, she was going to cry! He hadn't meant to be so blamed harsh. He turned away and stared at his tractor, praying she'd get a handle on her emotions. He turned back around just as she rubbed a tear off her cheek. Worried that anything he said at this point would only make things worse, he kept silent, letting the crickets fill the uncomfortable moment.

"I just don't get you," she said at last.

He rubbed the back of his neck and tried to think of the right response to make. He wasn't a mean guy. He didn't enjoy being in this position. "Look, Applegate told me you've wanted to be an actress ever since you were a little girl. And believe me, I wish you all the best. I'm really sorry you had to go through all of that as a child."

Her eyes flashed. "I didn't ask you to feel sorry for me. I asked you to help me put on a show."

"I don't feel sorry for you."

She glared at him, her eyes calling him a liar.

The woman made him crazy. "Okay, I *lied.* I'd be a jerk if I didn't feel sorry for you, and you know it."

"Don't worry about it—you're being enough of a jerk without bringing my childhood into the mix."

Ross was done. He clamped his mouth shut and didn't retaliate.

"What am I doing?" she asked as color drained from her complexion. "I'm sorry."

He didn't say anything as she backed toward the barn door.

"I have to go," she said. "I shouldn't have come out here. You don't want to do the show. That's your prerogative." She reached the entrance and stopped. "I don't know what I was thinking. I arrived here in Mule Hollow so certain that God had opened this door and that this was the right move for me." She paused, then shook her head, looking vulnerable. "Obviously, you are not part of that open door and I have harassed you enough." She clamped her lips shut, nodded as if to say goodbye and then turned and walked away.

Ross didn't move. He felt awful about the entire encounter and almost wanted to go after her. But he didn't.

Nothing had changed. She could call him what she wanted, but the truth was she would use this town and then drop it. She hadn't even tried to deny the fact.

Chapter Six

When Ross stepped onto the church grounds the next morning, Norma Sue and Esther Mae just about mowed him down as they barreled toward him, both of them hotter than an August wind during a drought.

"Of all the selfish, unbelievable things to do," Norma Sue said, breathing hard, her fists balled on her hips. "I'm of the mind that you have something against this girl."

"Really, Ross Denton, I'm ashamed of you. That barn is just rotting away out there," Esther Mae added. Her face was as pink as her hair was red, from anger as well as from her and Norma Sue's fifty-yard rush.

"Look, ladies, if I thought this idea of Sugar's would work, I might give in. But I don't think she stands a chance putting on something that big." He listened to them politely, but as soon as he could move on, he did. Only to be cornered by Applegate, Stanley and Sam.

"It ain't right you keepin' that poor little gal away

from her dreams," Applegate snapped, and his buddies agreed.

Poor little gal. "Can none of you see that Sugar has no earthly idea what she's getting herself into?"

Stanley scratched his bald spot. "Well, shor we kin. But what if she had some help? Do ya thank she could do it?"

"Yeah, what about that?" Sam added, elbowing in between his buddies so he could look up at Ross.

Ross surveyed the men, their wizened old eyes pushing him to "cowboy up."

"Look, fellas. We're talking lights, sound system, people to run them both. And that's only the beginning. Where is the audience going to sit? A stage would have to be built, plus she'd have to get costumes and props. It takes manpower, money, and let me say once more, it takes *commitment.* That's not even talking about the time that would have to be invested in rehearsals. Don't you see, we aren't talking about getting ready for a one-time weekend play. We're talking about a review-ready production that'll run weekend after weekend for months. She won't be sticking around long enough for it to benefit anyone but herself. So why should I work this into my schedule and commit to it when I don't have the time, or the desire? Especially since she'll leave the first minute Hollywood gives her a holler. Sorry, but no thank you. If you men want this so much for her, then y'all help her." He finished his harangue and stalked off, feeling like the bad guy once more. But *someone* needed to use his head around here. That's what he'd been telling himself all night long.

I arrived here in Mule Hollow so certain that God had opened this door and that this was the right move for me.

His gut clenched as her words came back to him. They had stuck with him long after she'd driven off last night.

She thought God had a plan for her here. She'd sounded so sincere.

He'd thought the same thing when he'd given up the stage and moved to the ranch. This was the place he was supposed to be, and no one could convince him otherwise. But they were different. He wasn't leaving.

His steps slowed when he saw Sugar across the church lawn. She looked like a rainbow in her colorful sundress, and she was surrounded by cowboys—obviously she held no grudge against *them* for turning down her show.

He knew all those cowboys, and knew that if there was a feasible way for them to help her, they would. She laughed at something one of them said, and Ross's chest tightened. He tried to shake it off as he entered the sanctuary. He reminded himself that he needed to keep his head on straight.

Not in a sociable mood, he grunted a greeting to those who spoke to him, then slumped into the first empty pew he could find in a far corner of the church. He could not let this woman get to him. He didn't want anything to do with a production, and he shouldn't feel bad about that.

But he did.

And there was just no getting around the fact that it bothered him how those other cowboys had turned her down, too, and yet they were out there getting smiles, while he'd gotten chewed out. Ross crossed his arms and watched the cowboys file into the choir loft a few minutes later. Norma Sue and Esther Mae took their seats in the center of the front row and smiled out at the congregation.

They did not smile at him.

Sugar had watched Ross out of the corner of her eye as he practically stormed toward the church and disappeared inside. She hadn't missed the fact that he'd been in what looked like a heated conversation with Norma Sue and Esther Mae, and then Haley's grandfather and his two buddies.

Sugar didn't know what the older men were getting on him about, but she could well imagine after last night that Norma and Esther were taking up for her.

She wanted to feel satisfaction. Oddly, she didn't.

She felt self-conscious, too, wondering if everyone in town knew her story. There was a chance that Applegate hadn't told everyone about her life, but she had a bad feeling that might not be the case. She despised pity. She'd lived with it for years, been coddled to death because of it. When she told people about how she got her name, she usually skimmed over the fact that the complications from her birth hadn't been resolved for years. Skimmed over her childhood as a lonely little girl who desperately prayed that God would give her a strong body someday.

She felt weak when people could see deep into her soul.

Last night, when she'd realized that Ross knew, she'd

behaved badly, in part because she really wanted to crawl under a rock. Pity was the last thing she wanted from him. She'd told the truth when she said she'd find a different place for her show. She didn't need him. But that hadn't stopped her from going home depressed or from hearing that horrible voice of defeat telling her to give up on her dreams.

That voice bothered her more and more. She'd thought for certain that she'd left it back in L.A. That it wasn't the Lord asking her to "lay down" her dreams. She wouldn't, couldn't think that God would ask such a thing of her. After all, He'd put these dreams in her heart. He *had.* And there was no way she'd quit just because achieving them was hard. She knew hard. She knew struggle.

She'd overcome adversity from the start of her life by believing she had a purpose. She was supposed to be a star, just like ones she'd watched as a child, the ones who'd filled her days with joy. She knew she was supposed to do the same thing. She was supposed to be America's next sweetheart. One who would bring joy to other little girls with dreams of their own. Some—many, actually—thought her dreams were trivial. But she would not give up.

She'd finally gone to sleep the night before determined to keep believing that she was supposed to be in Mule Hollow. But she would be lying if she claimed that all the adversity she was meeting wasn't pulling her down. Ross Denton was number one on that list. Did that stop her silly eyes from seeking him out as she took a seat in a pew near the back of the church? Oh no, it did not.

She could see his profile quite clearly. And what did she see?

The lump on his forehead!

It probably wasn't big enough for anyone else to notice, but because she knew it was there, she saw it clearly, even from a distance. Unwanted guilt settled on her and she looked away.

She was glad when a pretty brunette with a warm smile asked to sit beside her.

"Oh, please do." She scooted down the pew, so grateful for the distraction that she could have hugged the woman.

"Thanks. I'm Molly Jacobs. You must be Sugar," she said, sinking onto the seat and holding out her hand.

"I am!" Sugar exclaimed, instantly excited. "You are just the person I've been hoping to meet."

Molly chuckled. "Well, that makes two of us. I would have looked you up sooner, but I was out of town on a story. We have a lot to talk about, don't we?" she whispered, leaning in as Adela started playing the piano. "How about lunch at my house after church? I'd love to visit with you and learn all about this production I hear you want to start."

"I would love that!" Sugar's heart lifted. It was as if God had once again given her encouragement just when she needed it. He might not be making her dreams come true easily, but she knew He was on her side. And if God was on her side, then anything was possible...*anything!*

Like the fact that Bob, Molly's husband, really did sing like Tim McGraw. When the guy stepped out of the choir and began singing, Sugar noticed right away that he had a voice very similar to the country-music superstar's. Not only that, but he was backed up by a choir made up predominantly of cowboys who'd turned her down the night before. To her surprise, they had greeted her this morning with warm apologies, leaving her hoping that they might be able to work something out, after all. Her heart's hopes were renewed once more as she sat in the pew and listened to the music. Mule Hollow had talent.

Maybe Norma Sue was right. Sugar just needed a show where she was the central star, with only a few cast members that could be rotated in and out. Cowboy singing during the intermission and before the show would also be rotated. She was so excited about the renewed fire burning inside of her that she pretty much smiled through the entire service.

By the time she got home later that afternoon, the voice of doubt had been pushed far, far away. She and Molly had clicked instantly. The spirited reporter loved her idea of producing a show, and had promised to help all she could. She planned to start mentioning Sugar's idea in her column the very next week, even though Sugar didn't have anything completely pinned down.

Bob had promised to help, too, if she could come up with a rotating schedule, as she'd proposed. The handsome, completely-in-love cowboy had suggested a romance, since that was what Mule Hollow was all about, and to inspire her, he'd picked up his guitar and sung a love song to Molly. It was the most romantic thing Sugar had ever witnessed, and in spite of herself, she was inspired by the couple's relationship.

Molly had dreamed of being a journalist on foreign soil before she'd met Bob. That unsettled Sugar a bit, though their connection was undeniable. Both Haley and Molly had forfeited exciting careers for love. And while Sugar had a problem with women sacrificing their dreams for love, she couldn't deny that they both looked blissfully happy.

Still, Sugar couldn't help but wonder about Molly's future. How would she feel in the years to come? Would she look back on her choices with regret?

Of course, Molly's life choices were none of Sugar's business. She was just grateful that the columnist wanted to support *her* dream.

The phone was ringing as she entered her apartment. Dropping her purse and sliding out of her heels, she grabbed the portable receiver.

"Hey, sis, how are you?" her brother asked.

"Cody, it's good to hear your voice…is something wrong?"

"No, don't get in a panic. We were all over at Mom and Dad's for lunch after church today, and no one had heard from you, so we're checking in."

"Are you there now?" With Cody's words, she felt that familiar longing for family. Though she was hurt that none of them fully supported her decision to become an actress, she still missed them. She got her answer when a loud "hello" was shouted in unison over the phone line. She laughed, and tears threatened suddenly. "Hello, tell everyone hello."

"I'll let you do that yourself in a minute. I'm going to

pass the phone around, but first I'm going to get on to you. Why haven't you called and let us know you were settled?"

"I'm sorry." She knew she should have called. But she also knew they'd have tried once more to talk her into moving home. They always did. Always. "I'm here and it's a lovely place. I think you would approve of it." What was there not to approve of? If they wanted her to be in a safe location, this was it. Certainly it was safer than the neighborhood she'd been able to afford in L.A.

"Anyplace has to be better than where you were."

"Come on, Cody, don't start. Please." L.A. was just as safe as any other city, but they'd hated the thought of her being there.

"I'm not. But look, do you need any money?"

"No. I don't." They were constantly trying to give her money, and didn't like that she drove the same car she'd bought for almost nothing five years earlier. But Sugar was determined to make it on her own. So far, she'd been able to. The money she'd inherited from her grandmother had helped. But four overprotective, successful brothers were hard to hold off. They didn't seem to get that she had her pride, and that she'd decided that if none of them wanted to support her dream, she certainly wasn't going to let them support her financially. That wasn't going to happen even if they suddenly came around and started believing in her.

"Look, Cody, I'm making it on my own."

"I know, sis. I know," he grumbled, causing her to smile.

She spent the next thirty minutes talking with everyone in her family and enduring much of the same conversation over and over again. Still, when she hung up, she was grinning. God bless them, they meant well. But no matter what they thought, she was going to make it. She *was,* and she just wished in her heart that they'd believe in her.

Feeling restless and more determined than ever, she went down to the office to research one-woman-show ideas on the Internet. She had to come up with the show, but so far she hadn't liked anything she'd found. Nothing felt right.

And besides, she needed something with singing cowboys.

Chapter Seven

❧

"So what do you think, guys?" Sugar asked the bunch at the diner the next morning. It was only seven o'clock but she had been too restless to stay in her apartment, so had headed over to visit with Applegate, Stanley and Sam. "What should I do about a place to have my show?"

"We think you need ta git in yor car and go out thar and talk to Ross one more time," Applegate said loudly.

"That's right," Sam agreed. "Y'all have gotten off on the wrong foot, that's all."

"Yup," Stanley said. "He's just slap crazy right now 'cause of them critters destroy'n' his property. Did you know the beavers are tryin' ta turn his prime graz'n' land into a lake?"

Sugar was startled. She hadn't realized that Ross might be having personal problems. Suddenly, she remembered that he had been working on his tractor on Saturday night, too. "You think that might be one reason he's been so hardheaded?"

The three men nodded. Applegate met her gaze with a solemn look. "The boy jest needs some help out thar."

Stanley paused, a checker in hand. "He was in here first thang this mornin' on his way out thar. He needs help, all right. Everybody else is tied up with thar own work and cain't lend a hand."

Sam looked grim. "We'd go help, but, well, we're old."

"Yep, old as dirt," Applegate grunted.

On to them now, Sugar bit back a smile. They were totally up to something…but they still had a point. She had awakened this morning thinking maybe she should try once more to speak to Ross. The two of them had ended things on a horrible note on Saturday night and it didn't feel right. For goodness sakes, they were both Christians. But were these fellas up to no good? "So you think I should go out there and see if he needs some help? Me?"

They nodded again, looking pitiful. She actually thought they tried to frown so that more wrinkles showed on their faces. She bit her lip harder and breathed in through her nose, trying not to laugh. "Where are the beavers?" she managed to say, though her voice was a bit higher than normal. Not only would helping him give her the opportunity to show him a different side of herself, but she was actually curious about the beavers. She'd never seen one in real life.

Applegate grinned. "It's easy. Follow that road past his old barn and head through them trees and you'll find him."

As it turned out, she didn't have to drive to the beavers

to find him. She saw him coming out of his barn—aka her soon-to-be theater—as she approached. She pulled to a halt, and he paused halfway into his truck, with one foot on the floorboard and a hand on the door. He didn't seem happy to see her. Poor guy probably thought she was here to harass him again.

She hurried toward him. "I'm so glad I found you."

"Sugar, I don't have time for this now."

"I know you're having trouble with some beavers. The crew at Sam's told me."

His brows dipped beneath the shadow of his hat. "And why did they tell you that?"

"So I could come help you."

"What?" He scowled.

"Look, Ross. I feel horrible for the way things got out of line the other night. I've been thinking about it a lot and I'm really sorry. I came to help."

He shook his head. "I'm sorry, too. I'm not normally a bad guy. There are some things that I could have said differently. But you still can't use the barn, and I don't need your help." He sat down behind the wheel and closed the door. "Have a nice day," he said through the open window.

Sugar wasn't about to give up. She ran to the passenger door and yanked it open. "Whoa there, cowboy," she said, hopping inside. "You're not getting rid of me that easily. I'm coming with you."

"You are one stubborn woman," Ross said. "Fine. You want to come along so badly, then here we go. But it doesn't mean I'm changing my mind."

"Fine. But a girl has to have hope," she retorted, winning her a chuckle that sent good vibrations straight to her heart.

"So, you like the country?" she asked as they pulled back onto the gravel road and headed toward the trees. As soon as the words were out of her mouth, she winced. Small talk seemed awkward after their heated conversations, but she was trying to start over. Still, did she have to ask such a no-brainer? Not only had he already told her that he liked it here, but it was obvious. He fit the part to perfection.

"Yeah, I do," he said. "So, tell me, Sugar. Where are you from? Other than the land of glitz."

This was good. Friendly conversation. "Scottsdale, Arizona."

He seemed surprised, and glanced at her. "Why didn't you go back home to do this show?"

"My parents and brothers still live around there. Being the baby, I find they tend to smother me. Plus, Haley wanted me here, and Molly's column offers me a great advantage I couldn't get anywhere else."

"So how did you end up in Hollywood?"

This was really good; he was actually trying to get to know her. This was more like the first day they'd met. "I packed up my car and headed out right after high school. Big dreams have a tendency to disappear if you don't act on them early."

They were driving through the trees, and Sugar could see how the morning sunlight shot through the leaves like shafts on the road ahead of them. It was beautiful.

"So how far to these cute little beavers you want to run off your property?"

"Not far to where those furry nuisances are making a lake out of perfectly good grazing land."

She stared at the cows. There were some black ones and some gray ones, some with humps, some with horns. "They do look like they need a lot of room. Those are seriously big cows."

He shot her an amused glance. "You really aren't a country girl."

"Nope. I'm having real withdrawal problems out here. Oh," she gasped as the ground beside the gravel road they were driving on suddenly turned soggy. It was like lowlands after a flood. "This isn't normally like this?"

"A week ago, there were cattle standing out there, eating. If this keeps up, if the beavers get more trees down and block the creek's flow completely, the water will be over the road soon."

Now she could understand his displeasure with the animals.

They carried on through a small swath of trees and arrived at the creek, where a dam was built from branches and limbs. "That is amazing! Animals did that? Wow."

"That 'amazing wow' of a dam is a work of destruction." Ross parked the truck and got out.

Sugar followed. Wanting a closer look, she started walking toward the structure. The damage to the grove was obvious; tree stumps were everywhere.

"Look at that," she said, pointing…as if he hadn't already seen it. "And to think they did it with their teeth."

She lifted her finger and rubbed her incisors. "That must be some powerful enamel."

"Obviously," Ross grunted in disgust.

"What are those?" She pointed to some trees that had what looked like wire wrapped around them.

"Cages to keep the beavers from taking the tree down. Once I realized they'd moved in here, I had to start defensive action to try and save what I could. It's unbelievable what they can do in a single night."

"Is it working?"

"Not as well as I'd hoped. They get to them faster than I can wrap them."

As Sugar approached, she saw that in the flooded pond above the dam was a tall mound made of sticks and mud. "Is that where they live?" she asked, moving in for a closer look. She'd read that beavers live in a lodge rather than in their dam.

"I wouldn't go any closer than that. They could be in there and might think you're threatening them."

Suddenly, one surfaced! It popped up and, with its cute little ears moving in the water like tiny shark fins, circled in a wide, slow arc toward the shore. Its water-slicked head glistened in the morning sunlight.

"Look at him," she cooed, bending forward. Behind her, she heard Ross tell her to step back, but she didn't have time. One minute the beaver was in the water the next it launched itself from the water toward her like a deranged ninja!

Sugar screamed and stumbled back as the very angry, hairy wet beaver landed in front of her, combat ready—

talking in a language she couldn't understand. Mini Rambo charged her. From this angle, there was nothing cute about him. He was like a giant rat coming at her, teeth gnashing, and all Sugar could think as she started to fall was, "This is your due for coming to the country!"

It happened quickly. One minute, she was beaver bait as it latched its pearly whites onto her flip-flop, barely missing her toe as it snatched the shoe, tossed it to the side and headed for her. Dead meat for certain, Sugar was crab-crawling backward on her elbows when Ross swung her up into his capable arms.

"Yah!" he yelled, stomping hard with his boot, the spurs adding a tinkle to the pounding. The beaver stopped, squinted, then apparently decided that picking on girls was an acceptable practice, but big strong cowboys who yelled really, really loud were off-limits. Whatever its thoughts, Sugar was not complaining. Oh, no. Not this girl. Her brain was focused entirely on the arms wrapped securely around her and the hard chest that she found herself cradled against.

It was the best near-disaster she'd ever suffered through…*suffering* being hardly the correct term. She didn't even say anything when Rambo took her shoe with him as he slid back into the water. How could she when she looked up and found Ross nearly nose to nose with her, staring into her eyes? Rambo could have her shoe! He could have both, for that matter. Time clicked into fairy-tale speed, slowing, while her heart slammed against her chest like a sledgehammer. She thought she felt Ross's do the same beneath her palm, which rested over his heart.

The country had never looked so good.

"*That* was about the dumbest move I've ever seen," he snapped, stomping away from the dam toward his truck, and effectively erasing her ridiculous romantic image.

"What?"

"That was about the dumbest, most foolhardy thing I've ever seen," he repeated, practically dropping her beside the truck.

"I didn't mean for you to repeat it," she growled.

"Then why'd you ask?" His eyes were slits beneath the shadow of his hat.

She flapped her hands in exasperation and embarrassment. She knew every word he said was the truth. It had been a stupid move on her part, but after that outburst of his, she would never admit it to him. "For your information, I've never been around a beaver dam, much less a beaver. He was cute. I didn't realize he would pull a 'Teenage Mutant Ninja Beaver' act."

Still scowling at her, as if she were dumber than the fence posts lining the pasture, Ross rammed his hat brim with a knuckle, pushing it off his forehead. His eyes glittered as he glared at her.

And then it happened. She got a mental picture of the entire incident in her head…and she giggled. *Oh, brother,* she thought, as another chuckle escaped. She clamped a hand over her mouth, but it didn't help. It really was funny.

Of course, it came as no big surprise that he wasn't finding her giggles amusing. His eyebrows dipped. His eyes fogged with consternation, and when his jaw muscles tensed, she couldn't help but laugh out loud.

"This is not funny," he snapped, even as his lips twitched.

"Yeah, right," she sputtered, before hooting with laughter again. He was looking at her like she'd lost her marbles. Maybe she had, but she couldn't help it. "You," she finally managed to say, "were so cute rescuing me—"

"You could have been hurt. He almost took off your toe!"

She sucked in a deep breath, regaining control. "He stole my favorite flip-flops," she said, then giggled once more. "Took it back home to the little missy."

Ross bit his lip. She knew he wanted to laugh and she pushed for it when she batted her eyes and sighed, "You're my *hero*."

"Not hardly," he chuckled.

She shook her head as she waggled a finger at him. "You can't deny it after this. I owe you now."

He frowned. "You don't owe me anything."

"Oh, but I *do*. You know, in some countries, after someone has saved another person's life, that person is always indebted to them." She couldn't help teasing him.

"I did *not* save your life," he snapped, glaring at her.

She fought off another giggle. The man was too cute. "How do you know? I think you did. He wouldn't have stopped with my shoes. That horrible, horrible creature could have sliced me up like a hunk of baloney."

"Baloney! I got you before that happened."

She chuckled again. "I think you are just very modest." She tapped his chest. "I think you know that I very nearly lost my life back there," she said, her hand sweeping to her heart dramatically. She new she was pushing, but really the man was adorable all bowed up and terrified that she might start following him around from here to eternity, trying to repay the debt she owed him. She couldn't help stretching out his discomfort.

He sidestepped toward the truck. "I'm taking you back to your car. Don't you have work to do?"

"At ten. It's only seven-thirty."

"Are you always this much of an early riser?"

"You mean am I always a pest? Could be. Sleep is overrated. I function on about five hours a night. I'm on explore mode right now. So following you around every morning trying to repay my debt is going to work right into my schedule."

That won her a glare. The cowboy was really grand like that. She might just have to keep him riled, so she could enjoy seeing him all fierce and exasperated. And being the only girl in a family of four brothers, she could pick and pester with the best of them.

"Get in the truck."

She crossed her arms. "Nope."

"Sugar, you don't have but one shoe. How are you going to help me? Besides, the one shoe you have is a flip-flop. You can't work out here in girl shoes."

She laughed. "I'll use those," she waved toward the rubber boots that were turned upside down and stuck between the cab and the bed of his truck.

"Those will swallow you."

"I'm not going anywhere. Give me the boots."

He looked mad enough to eat nails. "This isn't working, you know. I am not going to give in and let you have my barn."

She held out a hand. "Boot, please. I have to help my *hero*."

"Would you stop that?"

"Nope. I owe you, and I always pay my debts, so let me help."

He scowled and reached for the boots. Oh yeah, she'd won. Still she smiled innocently.

He dropped his chin to his chest and she could feel his pain. She loved it.

Chapter Eight

Looking down at his boots, Ross drew in a deep breath and then blew it out slowly. He wanted to believe that thinking Sugar was going to land in the creek had him all shook up—and it *had* scared him, but holding her in his arms was what still had him rattled.

She had him at a disadvantage, turning on that smile and those dimples, along with the funny wit he'd noticed that first day.

"Okay, I'm ready," she said.

She'd pulled on his seven-sizes-too-big-for-her boots and stood smiling at him. She was having entirely too much fun at his expense. "If you say so," he growled, turning to the truck. He could hear her chuckling behind him, and despite himself, he smiled. He tugged on his gloves and strapped on his tool belt, all the while trying to ignore that Sugar had walked up beside him and was peering into the bed of his truck.

"That looks like a lot of wire. How many trees are you planning to cage?"

He smiled at her word choice. "A few," he said, as he grabbed the roll of galvanized fence wire. "Watch your step in those boots," he cautioned, then headed toward a tree. She followed at a slower pace.

He wanted to tell himself he wasn't enjoying her company, but that would be a lie. Fact was, this was what he prayed for. Not Sugar necessarily, but a wife who would enjoy getting out on the ranch and working beside him. Of course, he knew Sugar was just trying to soften him up so she could get what she wanted. And while that put a crimp in his contentment, the truth was he *had* softened up a little. Not that he would tell her. He wouldn't want to give her false hope. He wasn't changing his mind.

He dropped the wire and unrolled a section before cutting it the right length to go around the tree trunk. He pulled it up, then moved to the tree, where he'd already installed stakes the day before. He didn't need any help, and could only guess the conspiring old fellas' motives for convincing Sugar that she should come to his rescue. Still, as he wrapped the wire around the tree, he decided to humor her. "Can you hold the two ends together for me?" he asked.

"Sure thing," she said, moving close.

He immediately realized that humoring her wasn't such a good idea, after all. Man, but the woman smelled great. "So tell me why you want to be an actress," he blurted out, needing something to remind him of why letting her get too close wasn't a smart thing to do. "It's a hard life." He grabbed wire ties from his belt, and needle-nose pliers, and promised himself that no matter what this morning held, he was going to stick to his guns. He had to keep his head straight where Sugar Rae Lenox was concerned.

Sugar tried to concentrate on Ross's question, but the truth was, it was difficult. There was no denying that she was attracted to him. She couldn't help it. But she sucked in a deep breath and vowed to keep her eyes on her objective: making friends with him, and praying that God would change Ross's mind for her. Because truly, that was where her hope lay. All she could do was be herself.

Of course, she was used to his question. She'd been asked it so many times that she sometimes got a little miffed by it. But not today.

"People look at me like I'm crazy to want something so much. Something that is such a long shot. But I feel it, here." She put her hand on her heart, then touched her temple. "And here. It's not like it's just a whim. I went into it knowing the odds were against me. Knowing that the average actor makes below minimum wage and has to have a second job to actually pay the rent.... But still, I had to do it."

The corners of his mouth tilted up, but he didn't say anything, just nodded. Almost as if he got it, which made her plunge in, full speed ahead, trying to help him understand. In understanding, there was hope.

"I'm listening. Go on," he said.

"I can't really explain it. My parents…" She took a breath. "You know I said I'd tell you the story behind my name? Well, if you have the time, this is a good place to tell you."

"I have all the time in the world and I'm really interested. But I still want to hear the rest of the story on what drives you to be an actress."

"Oh, you will. In a way it's all intertwined."

He paused to smile at her. "Hit me with your best shot. I'm all ears."

Normally, she told the short version of her story. But since he already knew some of it, she decided to be open. And of course, this was all about building a friendship. That meant opening up and sharing. What could it hurt?

"See, I was born premature and wasn't given much of a chance of surviving. Sugar Ray was at his prime during that time, and the entire world was rooting for the lightweight champ…so because of the similarities in our last names, my parents started calling me Sugar, their little fighter. I was originally supposed to be Amanda Marie Lenox. Do I look like an Amanda Marie?"

He laughed and shook his head. "You look like Sugar Rae."

"That's right, I do," she declared. "Nothing against the names Amanda or Marie, I'm just Sugar Rae. Maybe I'm partial to my name because so many people were chanting it at me before I even weighed three pounds. But my mom says everyone in the hospital knew Sugar Rae was the tiny baby on the fourth floor fighting for her life. And they were all rooting and praying for me. I still have a couple of banners packed away back home that the nursing staff made, saying, 'Come on, Sugar Rae, you can do it!' My parents love to tell that story and how in addition to the nurses chanting it to me, people passing by the preemie wing could be heard saying it. And that was where it began…this quest. What started as an affirmation for me—wanting to fight like they told me—became a motto as I grew up. I started out a fighter for surviving. I've been surviving ever since. I had several complications that lingered and took years to correct, through countless operations as I grew older. Which meant that I spent a lot of time recuperating, sick at home, watching television."

Through with binding the wire, Ross gave her his full attention. "I think I get it. They helped you," he said, his voice thoughtful.

He understood. Sugar's throat tightened, but she struggled not to cry. She still didn't want his pity. "Yep," she said, copying Stanley. "Those terrific stars took a bored little girl to wonderful worlds of make-believe. I can't even remember the first time I said, 'I'm going to be a star.' It was just there, in my head and heart, as if it was supposed to be. My parents and my four brothers were all supportive when I was small. I didn't know that they thought the dream would eventually go away and I would decide what I really wanted to do with my life. But when I joined the drama club in high school and the choir, and then told my parents that I wanted to major in theater in college, they started to balk."

She paused and Ross looked at her encouragingly. "I

have the most wonderful family in the world, don't get me wrong, but I'm the baby girl, the little sis who's been through so much. They just didn't want to see me go into something with such a high rate of failure. They were, and are still, trying to protect me."

"I can understand that," Ross said, making no move to cut wire for another tree. Instead, he crossed his arms and asked, "So they still don't support you?"

It surprised her that it still hurt. She looked away, across the flooded pasture. "They pretend. But deep down they don't get it, and would rather I just come home." She met his attentive gaze. "They raised me to believe I could do anything if I set my mind to it...but without meaning to, they put those dreams inside a nice, neat box. I was supposed to grow up and pick my dreams out of that safe box."

Ross lifted a dark brow. "But you don't take the safe route to anything. You're Sugar Rae."

She smiled, feeling lighter at heart. "I try not to. But that's not really how I think. I just know that this is what I'm supposed to do. God has a plan for me, I know it. I just can't seem to get there." She didn't go into how she thought God was toying with her sometimes. How it felt as if He were holding a carrot out and watching her suffer as she tried to reach it. That sounded too negative, and she didn't want to give in to that feeling. "Failure isn't an option to me. I believe I'm meant to be an actress. And I know some people look at that as such a frivolous career. But, if God puts a song in your heart, I believe you should sing that song. This song has been in my heart from the beginning—how do I just stop singing? How do I walk away from something that is a part of me?"

She hadn't meant to take the conversation to such a deep level. Truth was, she hadn't ever shared that much of herself with anyone before, and it shook her up just a bit. But she couldn't seem to stop the flow. "I'm failing. I don't really understand how it's happening, but I am. Mule Hollow is my last shot. I was so close to making it many, many times, but something always fell through. Now even my agent is starting to think maybe he made a mistake and I'm not as special as he thought.

"There aren't many towns that have an award-winning columnist writing weekly columns about it. Because of Molly, and the publicity I thought I might be able to stir up if I got her on my side, I feel like this is where my dream can finally come true. I mean, what are the chances that my best friend happens to move back here and need my help at just the time that I've hit rock bottom? Or that when Haley called me for the job, I just happened to be drowning my sorrows in a tub of ice cream while watching Paul Newman's *Biography* talking about him being discovered while performing at summer stock?" Ross didn't smile, just nodded his head.

"Providence," Sugar declared. "That's what it is. And that's why I'm here. I just need to make a splash, get some great publicity, and I can make it happen."

"What if you do fail?"

Her heart sank at the question. This was the same old song and dance. But she wasn't letting fear inside her head again. "I told you, it's not an option."

Lay it down. The phrase echoed in her thoughts and she gritted her teeth against it. Meanwhile, Ross watched her, as if weighing his words and choosing carefully what he was going to say. She knew the look and prepared herself for the usual assurance that failure wasn't just an option, but a probability. Curtis, her eldest brother, was a lawyer, and he'd been the one to use that terminology. She didn't like it, even though he'd said it in kindness and frustration. In love.

But love was letting someone go, too, wasn't it? And they'd done that in the end, because she'd given them no choice.

"Success is a relative thing," Ross said. "One man's success is another man's failure. No one can really judge someone else's dreams. I believe you have to follow your own path…no matter what. It took me a while to realize that. I know a few actors and some great musicians who make a nice, stable living for themselves in Branson. They've managed to carve out successful careers and are famous in their own right as main attractions there. There are some that would think they've settled for less, that they failed because they didn't make it in Hollywood or Nashville. What do you think about that?"

"If that's their dream, then that's wonderful. I don't see anything wrong with it. But that's not my dream. That's not what I see—I see more. I know that sounds arrogant, maybe foolish."

She was shaken that she'd revealed so much. Exposed so much of herself to Ross, practically a stranger.

"Who is to say your dream is foolish? Who is to say

you won't make it? I've only known you for a short while, and frankly, I can't figure out why those powers that be in Hollywood haven't grabbed you up and put you in the movies. You're beautiful, you have an electric energy about you that I can't imagine them not connecting with. And you have the drive of twenty people."

Sugar's heart was thundering in her chest like a runaway herd of longhorns. "Wow. Thanks," she told him.

The left side of his mouth quirked. "Thought you had me all figured out, didn't you?"

She didn't think she would ever figure him out. "Actually, I was confused about you from the beginning," she said, making him chuckle. But it was true. She didn't understand him. But she suddenly knew that she would like to. This was dangerous stuff for a girl with no intentions of sticking around, no interest in forming ties to a place.

"C'mon. I had better get you back to your car so you can go to your real job."

He took her elbow and guided her toward the truck. The feel of his hand, sure and strong against her skin, made her keenly aware of him beside her. She almost let herself wish he would walk beside her every day....

It was not a feeling she'd ever felt before. It was scary and she didn't need it.

She needed his barn. And only his barn.

Chapter Nine

Sugar had just stepped up onto the sidewalk when Norma Sue and Adela came out of Heavenly Inspirations.

"What happened to your shoes?" Norma Sue called, heading her way.

Sugar waited for them to cross the street. She was barefoot and hoping she didn't get a splinter traversing the rough wooden sidewalk to the office. "A beaver stole one of my flip-flops so I took the other one off."

Adela placed a delicate hand over her heart. "A beaver stole your shoe?"

"One of Ross's beavers stole your shoe?" Norma Sue echoed, only louder and with a grin. "Those are some moody little whittlers. What were you doing out there? Trying to talk Ross into letting you use his barn?"

"Sort of. Applegate and Stanley—and Sam, too—they thought Ross needed some help, so I went out there," Sugar stated.

"*They* sent you to help Ross?" Norma Sue looked as skeptical as she sounded. She was a rancher herself, which was more than apparent from her clothes. Though she'd worn a dress on Sunday, Sugar hadn't seen her in anything other than denim the rest of the time. Usually she wore overalls and boots.

Sugar smiled at her. "They were really just trying to give me an excuse to talk him into letting me use his barn."

Adela smiled. "And did it work? Did he relent and agree?"

"I didn't ask him."

Norma Sue shook her head. "What were you thinkin', girl?"

"That's just it—I wasn't thinking." She laughed and filled them in on the details about the beaver: how Ross had rushed in like a hero and scooped her up, then scared the ninja beaver away. "After he was so gallant, I just couldn't harass him. Besides, like Adela said the other night, God's going to work this out for me. Although I have to tell you ladies, I am getting impatient."

Adela patted her arm. "You have the right attitude. Don't you worry, that boy is going to come around. We're going to pray some sense into him."

"Or badger it into him," Norma Sue added with a wide grin. "You just wait till I tell Esther Mae. She's out at No Place Like Home—you know, the women's shelter— babysitting right now, but she's going to enjoy your beaver adventure. And don't you worry, that boy is gonna come to his senses. Just you wait and see."

Sugar hoped they were right. She said goodbye, then hurried upstairs for a new pair of shoes. That cranky ole beaver had stolen her favorite flip-flop. The meanie. She got tickled again thinking about it and as she entered the office a few minutes later, it was still playing in her head. It would actually make a funny scene in a play.

Speaking of plays, she sat down and turned on her computer. She had real-estate business to take care of; updating the weekly ads for the area papers was her main priority today. But then she could read the plays her agent had e-mailed her.

She had to find something and soon. She'd been in Mule Hollow for a week now and had accomplished zero. She had to find the right play, so when Ross came through for her as she was praying he would, she would be ready.

The beaver scene popped into her head off and on all day. And when she started reading plays that afternoon, the silly beaver scene wouldn't let her concentrate.

By about eight that evening, she was really frustrated. It wasn't just the stupid beaver encounter that was distracting her. Now she had a whole bunch of thoughts churning around inside her head, begging her to write them down. Giving up on her reading, she headed upstairs. This was ridiculous. She was an actress, not a writer. It had never even crossed her mind before. But now that it had, maybe she'd give it a shot. At this point, she'd give anything a chance if it might lead to success.

On Sunday morning, Sugar's heart about jumped out of her chest when she saw Ross step into the hallway of the Sunday school wing. He hadn't attended the first hour the week before, so she hadn't expected him now. But she was glad to see him there. All week, she'd hoped he would call with the news that he'd had a change of heart. He hadn't. Of course, she knew that, like many of the ranchers, he was trying to get hay up before the rain fell yesterday. But still she'd wanted him to call.

Today, she was tired. She'd thrown herself into finding the perfect script, but nothing seemed right. Also, she was still distracted by the ideas in her head, and was attempting to write them down. They hadn't totally come together, and were more than a little intimidating…but at least they had shown her what type of production piece she wanted. That alone was a much-needed boost.

The sight of Ross walking toward her wiped away her bad mood. Her heart skipped inside her ribs and she knew she was grinning like a fool.

"Hello, stranger," she called, feeling promise in the air. "So how are our beavers?"

"Busy as usual. But I think they are starting to move downstream. I got the majority of trees covered up, and installed a device that changes the water flow, so things are looking up."

Sugar was about to ask him if he'd found her flip-flop when they moved, but she didn't get the chance before Esther Mae and Norma Sue spotted them and charged down the hallway.

Esther Mae swooped her into a hug, her outrageous hat making Sugar sneeze when the purple feathers tickled her nose.

"Ross Denton, shame on you," she said as she stepped away, giving Sugar room to breathe while she glared at Ross. "This girl could have lost a toe out there getting attacked by a beaver on your property. And all because you are being so stubborn."

Sugar was so startled by the outburst that she laughed. Ross, however, looked as if he might try to make a run for it. Norma Sue stepped sideways, effectively cutting off his escape route.

"All this nonsense needs to stop," she snapped, giving him a stern look of disapproval. "You need to let her use your barn and you need to do it now! Around here, we *help* each other. This poor girl almost lost a limb coming out there to help you fix your beaver problem. Now you need to reciprocate."

Norma Sue was peeved! She was positively fuming.

And Esther Mae, too. "That's right," she stated, nodding so hard her feathers shook. She pointed at Sugar. "Just you look at this beautiful girl. She wants to bring a smile to everyone's lives with a little entertainment, and you are making her work unnecessarily hard. Don't you want to see her sing and act for us? You are depriving all of us of a good thing, Ross Denton."

Sugar had to bite her lips to keep the smile inside. Ross, however, wasn't pleased. Exasperated—oh, yeah.

"Ladies, I think this is between Sugar and me."

Not a good thing to say. Norma Sue's eyes narrowed and she stepped up to him. He was well over six feet of lean, hard muscle, and Norma Sue was half his height and three times as round. When she poked her finger in his chest, she had to crane her neck to meet his startled eyes. "You are not funny, mister. That barn is sitting out there wasting away when *she*—" her thumb jerked Sugar's way "—wants to put it to good use."

By this time, the hall was filling up with people. Some scooted around their group. Some, mostly cowboys, watched Ross's predicament with interest, clearly finding it entertaining.

Ross was not so amused—he was really cute, looking all dark and a bit woebegone, Sugar decided.

"Now listen, Norma Sue, I'm not discussing this here. It's my barn. She can do her thing at the community center and then head back to Hollywood where she belongs."

Well, that sounded brutal. So much for making any forward progress with him! Sugar met his unflinching eyes and lifted one eyebrow, a feat that had taken her a long time to learn. For the sake of her art and the camera, in scenes that would call for an expression of disapproval, she'd spent hours in front of the mirror, practicing. She was very glad of that time spent now and knew exactly what he was seeing.

He didn't appear intimidated at all. On the contrary, he shook his head, excused himself, and instead of sidestepping Norma Sue, spun and stalked back down the hall and out the door.

That bothered Sugar, but Norma Sue looked at her with a sly smile of satisfaction. "There. That should do it," she said, and then she and an equally pleased Esther Mae hustled away.

Poor Ross was being bamboozled!

Sugar had seriously underestimated these deceptively innocent-looking ladies.

Boy, it was nice to have them in her corner. Better with her than against her. Poor Ross.

So the women thought they could manipulate him!

Ross stormed out onto the church lawn, still fuming. Most everyone was inside, settling into their classrooms, and he was thankful there was no one else to harass him as he stalked down the sidewalk toward the parking lot. He'd just turned the corner of the church when he almost mowed over Pastor Allen.

"Ross," he said. "Is something wrong?"

"Yes, sir, there is," Ross said honestly. "Pardon me, but today just isn't a day I need to be in the sanctuary." He started to move on, but the preacher put a detaining hand on his arm.

"I'd say by the sound of it that today is indeed the very day you need to be in church. How about you and I go into my office right now and talk about this? I've got forty minutes to fill before the service starts, and it looks to me like the good Lord just gave me an appointment." He smiled, and his eyes shone bright with encouragement.

Ross had always respected the dedicated preacher. When he'd taken on the job a few years back, he'd already retired to a piece of land about fifty miles north of town. But because Mule Hollow needed a preacher and couldn't keep one for any length of time, he would come out and preach whenever he was needed. Eventually, the church stopped trying to find a pastor and asked him to take the job full-time. He'd done so, while continuing to commute. His wife was in poor health and needed to be closer to her doctors. Ross had much respect for Pastor Allen for giving up part of his retirement for their community, when he obviously had plenty on his hands already.

But Ross had never really spent much time in the pastor's office, not being one to run to the preacher with his problems. He figured the man had enough on his plate. Today, however, Ross needed to talk to someone. "I'd appreciate that," he said, and followed Pastor Allen around the side of the annex to the private entrance to the offices.

Feeling awkward, he dropped into one of the chairs facing the desk as the robust preacher hurried around and took his seat. "So tell me, does this have to do with the nice young lady who wants to use your barn for a show?"

Ross laughed, taken by surprise. "Yes, sir. That's exactly what's wrong. I might help if I thought she was going to stick around, but she isn't. And I can't get anyone to see that. It's not like I don't feel for her, because I do. I mean, she irritates me, don't get me wrong. The woman gets under my skin and makes me feel plum crazy." He stopped abruptly, suddenly remembering he was talking to the preacher, who wouldn't want to hear about how Ross couldn't stop thinking of Sugar. But Pastor Allen cupped his hands together on his desk and smiled.

"Go on," he urged. "It sounds to me like you need to get this off your chest."

Boy, was that an understatement. "Fact of the matter is, I don't want to be involved in the entertainment business again, either. I don't want anything stealing my energy away from my ranch. Maybe that's selfish, but it's the way I feel." He didn't add that Sugar scared him with the way she made him think about doing just that.

"But even so, it makes you feel guilty."

"How did you guess?"

"You wouldn't be this upset if you didn't care. And because you care, you feel guilty."

Ross nodded. "I gave that life up. I didn't plan on it trying to follow me here. It isn't easy for me to say no when I feel empathy for her. She really does believe that this is part of God's plan for her life. It puts me in a very bad position, because I know how to help her. I just don't want to center my life around a show again. That's not my dream."

The pastor propped his fingers together and rested his chin against them as he thought. After a moment, he dropped his hands and met Ross's gaze with frank eyes. "I think you should look at it from a different angle. Do you have a desire for the Lord to use you?"

"Yes."

"You say that, but let me ask you this. Do you want the Lord to use you as He sees fit or as *you* see fit?"

That stung, and Ross didn't like it. He'd had his life planned out. He was going to ranch, marry a great woman and raise some kids. God could use him for that.

"I can't say what you should do," the pastor continued, "but I'd like to pray with you, and then I suggest you spend some time thinking about this with an open mind. You never know what blessings the Lord has waiting for you if you're willing to answer His call. But even more important than that, you never know who you are going to be a blessing to by putting their needs before your own."

Ross felt ashamed, especially with this coming from a man who'd blessed an entire community by giving up part of his retirement to minister to them on Sundays. He looked up at the ceiling and let out a long sigh of frustration. Could he do this? God was throwing him a curveball that he hadn't expected....

"You know, I can tell you this," Pastor Allen said. "I believe God gave you a talent. What if those twenty years performing in Branson were really just your preparation for His true purpose in giving you that gift?"

Ross sat up straight. "My grandpop used to say something similar." He took a deep breath and stood up. He needed more time to think. "Thank you," he said, holding out his hand.

Pastor Allen rose and took his hand with a firm grip. "Let's have that prayer before you go. And then, why don't you stay for the service?"

Sugar was surprised to see Ross sitting in the sanctuary when the service started. She'd been afraid he'd left after Norma Sue and Esther Mae's impromptu performance, and she'd felt guilty all through Sunday school. When she saw him sitting on the far side of the sanctuary, as he had the week before, she wanted to go over and apologize. But she didn't know if she'd be welcomed, so she sat a few rows back, beside Molly again.

Sugar was tired. And she felt the sting of guilt every time she glanced at Ross's back. She prayed during the service that God would lead her. It was an awkward prayer.

The sermon was on giving up your will for God's will, giving everything to God. Well, she was trying. All her life, she'd worked so hard to fulfill this dream she had, this purpose to which she felt God had called her. And it wasn't easy, especially when she felt He wasn't doing much to help.

When the last hymn was over, she looked across the church and was startled to see Ross moving toward her.

His beautiful emerald eyes were not happy, and that was worrisome, too. Was her dream supposed to make someone else so miserable? She said goodbye to Molly and a few other friends around her and waited for him to reach her. Her stomach felt like the inside of a blender as she waited for the inevitable confrontation.

He stopped in the aisle, holding his Stetson between both hands, his back ramrod straight. "Would you have lunch with me?"

It was the last thing she'd expected him to ask. She stared up at him and said the only thing that came to mind. "Okay."

Chapter Ten

Ross's house was lovely, older, with a neat yard and a beautiful patio made of sandstone and granite. She had a vivid picture of cozy gatherings with friends as she followed him across the terrace and into the kitchen.

He held the door open for her and she was all nerves as she brushed past him. He'd asked her to lunch, said they needed to talk, and she had agreed, hoping this was a good sign. But he'd been quiet on the drive out to his home, and that quietness had her feeling as if she'd stepped on stage without memorizing her lines.

His kitchen was spacious, with wood floors and walnut cabinetry. "You have a wonderful place," she said, wishing her insides didn't feel so twisted every time she looked at him.

"Thanks, I've done some work on it."

"You did this yourself?" She was startled. Ross didn't look like Mr. Fixit.

"Don't be so surprised. Cowboys like to use tools," he

said, and the tension between them seemed to ease a bit. He smiled at her. "Clint Matlock and I have a little competition going when it comes to outdoing each other."

Sugar looked at the kitchen with new eyes. "Wow, I'm impressed. Every time I think I might have you figured out, you prove me wrong."

"I feel the same way about you." He held her gaze with unsmiling eyes.

That look did erratic things to Sugar's heartbeat, and what little ease in tension she'd felt seconds ago dissipated right away.

He turned toward the sink. "Make yourself at home. Are steaks okay with you?"

"I love steak." Her voice sounded odd, too high. "But you could feed me a sandwich if you wanted to. That would get me out of your hair quicker."

He chuckled, and she almost wilted with relief. "I'm serious," she said, watching him wash his hands. The man really had nice hands, strong arms. She remembered how they felt wrapped around her when he'd saved her at the beaver dam…. Okay, so maybe she shouldn't think about those strong arms.

He looked straight at her. "I'll feed you steak."

How was it that a man telling her he'd feed her steak could please her so much? She smiled at him. "Okay. But put me to work. What can I do? And by the way," she added, feeling as if it needed to be said, "I didn't put Norma Sue and Esther Mae up to that this morning."

An awful thought occurred to her. He might be feeding her steak to soften the blow of telling her in no uncertain

Get 2 Books FREE!

Steeple Hill Books,
publisher of inspirational romance fiction, presents

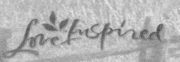

A series of contemporary love stories that will lift your spirits and reinforce important lessons about life, faith and love!

FREE BOOKS!
Get two free books by acclaimed, inspirational authors!

FREE GIFTS!
Get two exciting surprise gifts absolutely free!

2 FREE BOOKS

▲ To get your 2 free books and 2 free gifts, affix this peel-off sticker to the reply card and mail it today!

We'd like to send you two free books to introduce you to the *Love Inspired®* series. Your two books have a combined cover price of $11.00 in the U.S. and $13.00 in Canada, but they are yours free! We'll even send you two wonderful surprise gifts. You can't lose!

Each of your **FREE** books is filled with joy, faith and traditional values as men and women open their hearts to each other and join together on a spiritual journey.

GET 2 FREE BOOKS!

HURRY!

Return this card today to get **2 FREE Books** and 2 **FREE** Bonus Gifts!

Love Inspired®

YES! *Please send me the 2 FREE Love Inspired® books and 2 FREE gifts for which I qualify. I understand that I am under no obligation to purchase anything further, as explained on the back of this card.*

affix free books sticker here

313 IDL ERV5   **113 IDL ERVH**

FIRST NAME	LAST NAME

ADDRESS

APT.#	CITY

STATE/PROV.	ZIP/POSTAL CODE

Steeple Hill®

▼ DETACH AND MAIL CARD TODAY! ▼

® and ™ are trademarks owned and used by the trademark owner and/or its licensee.
© 2007 STEEPLE HILL BOOKS
(LI-LA-08)

terms that she couldn't use his barn. Kind of like a last meal or something. After all, he had been highly upset after being accosted by the ladies.

He nodded. "That's good to hear, but what do you say we not talk about that for now?"

"Okay. I just wanted you to know. So what can I do?" If he hadn't invited her over to talk about that, then she wasn't sure what they were doing. But oddly enough, she realized she was fine with that. She was curious about this man, and whether things went her way with his barn or not, she wanted to have this time to know him a little better.

"I'm not much of a salad guy, so there isn't anything in the fridge to fix one. But there's some canned stuff in the pantry if you want to go pick something out to go with steak and potatoes." He pointed toward the appropriate door.

"That sounds good to me," Sugar said, and headed that way, feeling a bit surreal about the entire situation. The pantry was a large walk-in with floor-to-ceiling shelves. In the dim light, she could see that one entire side was loaded with glass jars of food.

"The light switch is by the door on the left," he called.

"Thanks." She flipped the switch, and immediately let out a low whistle. "Whoa. This is some *serious* canning. Did you put all this up?" She was amazed by the jars. There were all sorts of things marked with various colored labels. Many of them appeared to be pickles: sour, dill, sweet, sweet and sour. There were also pickled pears, pickled peppers, pickled…she had to get up close to read that one…zucchini. There were icicle pickles, whatever in the world those were, squash pickles, pickled carrots, pickled relish, pear relish, cranberry relish, jalapeño relish, corn relish… Ross's chuckle finally interrupted her dazed inventory of his pickled goods. "Who are you? Peter Piper?" she asked.

"Looks that way. It's something, isn't it? My grandmother in Missouri is a canning queen, and the ladies here are, too. Cucumbers, squash and zucchini are things gardeners always have an overabundance of, so you see where it all ends up. If you think that's something, you should take a look at my freezer."

"You'll never eat all this. And if you even tried, you'd pickle yourself." Sugar grabbed a jar of green beans, unpickled, and a jar of squash, and went back to the kitchen.

"Tell me about it. My gram, she just keeps sending it. Doesn't want me to starve while I'm here without a wife." He shook his head. "It makes her happy, but when I get married I'm calling a halt to the canning thing. Take what you want when you leave, and stock your pantry. Although I'm surprised you haven't already started getting baskets of the stuff."

"Maybe it's just you cowboys that they want to keep from starving."

"Maybe. To tell you the truth, I'm not crazy about anything pickled."

They laughed and he prepared the steaks while she opened the jars and started heating the contents. Then they headed outside so he could fire up the pit. She'd never been much of a griller, and watched with interest as he got the fire going. She felt more at ease than she had before, and Ross seemed to relax, also.

"So your grandmother who sends you all this food, is she part of the show?"

He shook his head as he pulled the hood down on the pit. "No. She always said she married the talent. But her job is important. She oversees the costumes and runs the front office."

Sugar could hear the affection in his voice. "Don't get mad at me, but honestly, I still don't get how you could walk away from that."

He leaned against the porch rail and looped his thumb in the pocket of his jeans. "There are times when I miss it. After as many years as I spent up on that stage, it's to be expected. I was singing with Grandpop when I was four. But it stopped satisfying me. I wanted something of my own. Something that I built myself…. I got that from Grandpop. This is it for me. This ranch either makes it or it doesn't because of what I do. Of course, there's the God factor in the equation. He's got to be in the wagon with me, and I believe He is, but I'm willing to adapt if He throws me a curveball. I hope this is my final destination. I feel at peace here. A wife and kids will probably shake the peace up a bit, but should make it a whole lot more enjoyable."

Sugar could see that.

"So what if God decided to throw *you* that curveball?" he asked. "Are you ready to adapt if it means finding happiness?"

Why did she suddenly feel as if she was being tested?

"So you are about to tell me the same thing my parents tell me. That God probably isn't interested in my being an actress."

"Is that what they say?"

She walked to the porch railing beside him and studied the horizon. "Not in so many words. But they clearly don't support my dream. It's not in the safe box, remember." She couldn't hide her bitterness. "Acting is not considered worthwhile. It doesn't matter that movies give hours and hours of joy and entertainment to people."

"So there's a strain between you?"

Again she expelled a breath of frustration. They'd already talked about this, and she'd told Ross more than she'd ever told anyone. "No. They try to accept me, but there are small things that happen. Like they never came to visit me while I was in California. They always hint that I should come home. They're just waiting for me to fail."

She had her hand resting on the railing when Ross suddenly covered it with his and squeezed gently. Her stomach went bottomless. Though he let go almost immediately, the action touched her deeply.

"Maybe they're just worried about you." His voice was soft. "Like you told me the other day, you've chosen a field with a high rate of failure, full of intense stress and constant struggle. The rewards can be great one day and then gone the next. Your parents see what happens to stars in the tabloids. I'm sure it's hard on them. It's not exactly the same thing as going into teaching or medicine."

She felt an ache deep in her soul. "Yes, I understand that. I just wish they believed in me."

"I'm playing devil's advocate here, but might they simply be afraid for you?"

She gave a derisive laugh. "I'm afraid for myself at this point." She couldn't believe she'd just admitted that. And to Ross, of all people.

"And that is why I'm asking the hard question again. What if you don't make it? Isn't it time to think about that possibility? What if you have God's intentions mixed up with your own?"

Again, she had that sense of being tested. She thought of the voice of doubt that kept coming out of the shadows, telling her to lay it down. "I don't. And I won't quit. I refuse to believe that all these years were wasted. That *He* put this desire inside me only for it to mean nothing. That's not acceptable to me. Besides, there's that Bible verse that says He will give us the delights of our hearts. This *is* the delight of my heart. Plus, despite all the things that haven't gone my way since I arrived, producing the show here feels right. It just seems like I'm supposed to be *here*. I know this is my last shot, but I *feel* like it's the right one. Do you understand that? All I need is a little help—from you."

He studied her for a long moment. "So, what would you say if I agreed to let you use the barn?"

Time stopped, as if the world were holding its breath. She wanted this so much, it was almost too hard to believe. Ross had sounded so against it with all those questions he'd asked. Was he finally about to relent?

"Seriously?" she asked. The ladies had winked at church, all sure of themselves, but truly, Sugar had begun to think he wasn't ever going to come around.

He nodded. "Like a herd of women have been pointing out to me, it *is* just sitting there, wasting away. Waiting on a second life." He smiled.

She reacted with delight and relief, flinging her arms around his neck and squeezing him tight. "Thank you! *Thank* you!" she squealed in his ear. His arms went around her and he hugged her back, laughing at her excitement. She just couldn't believe it.

Could *not* believe it.

"Hey," he chuckled against her hair. "You might not thank me once you hear my terms."

Terms?

Chapter Eleven

"Terms, terms, who cares? You're the best, Ross Denton." She looked up at him, realizing that she'd just thrown herself into his arms. Judging by the expression on his face, he was just as surprised as she. His arms tensed around her and she noticed they were close enough to kiss. Her eyes drifted to his lips, the moment stalled and every thought vaporized into thin air.

Oh, no, girl! She pulled back and he let her go easily. But as she moved away from him, her thoughts were spinning. And to her dismay, she wished for nothing more than to feel his arms around her, pulling her close again as he kissed her.

Crazy. Crazier than crazy. Now more than ever, it was imperative that she maintain a professional relationship.

"My terms are," he said, clearing his throat and raking a hand through his hair, "that I'll help, but you'll have to take my advice. Because I still don't believe you have the slightest notion about what you are getting yourself into."

That was no joke, she thought, as her eyes cried mutiny and dropped to his lips. "I agree," she finally said. At that moment, she'd agree to anything. The man was letting her use his barn. That was all that mattered. She focused, and took a deep breath. She wasn't worried. She would be able to get him to see things her way once they got going. The key thing was just getting started.

For that alone she wanted to kiss him.

Who was she kidding—she just wanted to kiss him, period.

And that was not happening. No way. Not at all.

"Well, I guess you should check those steaks and I had better go check on those pickled prunes, or whatever it is I put on the stove. And—and then we can talk." She hurried away as if she were being chased by a pack of beavers.

"If there are prunes in there, you're on your own," he called after her.

"Hey, I'm so happy right now that I might eat them."

On Monday morning, everyone was buzzing about Ross teaming up with Sugar.

"Now I just have to convince him to be the hero in my production," she announced.

Haley groaned from across the office. "You are relentless. The poor guy doesn't know what he's unleashed. But I have to say that I think you and him together on stage would be a combustible duo."

Even though she was thinking the same thing, Sugar snapped shut the file she was going through and gave her boss a "don't even think about it" look. She was hoping the message would translate to her own brain. *Stop thinking about it!*

"You know you like him. I can see it in your eyes when y'all argue."

Sugar took heart in the truth. "That is exactly it. We don't see eye to eye much. And I'm afraid this new venture is going to get pretty heated sometimes. The man may have finally given in, but the fact remains that he is mule stubborn."

"Ha. And you aren't?"

"Well, *yeah,* I'm stubborn, but so what? I don't believe that stuff about how much fun making up can be."

Haley rolled her eyes and opened the door to leave. "Believe me when I tell you that making up is a *lot* of fun. But that's not the point, and you know it. If you would give him half a chance, you might find out how much y'all have in common."

Oh, she was more tempted to do just that. More tempted than she could afford to let herself admit. But she wasn't about to let Haley know that, so she just grunted. "What? That I want to be an actor and he doesn't?"

"Well, maybe you're right about that. But I can't help thinking you two might actually find some happy medium in all of this. Okay, gotta fly."

Haley hurried to her car and Sugar went back to work. But she couldn't help glancing at the clock first. Just a few more hours, and then she was meeting Ross at the barn. *Her* barn. She could barely contain herself, just thinking about it.

An hour or so later, Applegate and Stanley came into the office. They stopped just inside the doorway and fidgeted, reminding her of two little boys. "Mornin', Sugar," they said almost in unison, and nearly blew out the windows. Apparently, neither had their hearing aids turned on.

"Good morning. What can I do for you fellas?"

"It's what we can do fer you," Applegate barked.

"Yup, you tell her, App," Stanley said, nudging him with an elbow.

"Fer these here shows, you were a talkin' about how you were gonna need lights, right?"

Sugar nodded. "Sure." She hoped to locate some large spotlights soon. She had a friend in L.A. scouting out used ones.

"And you need somebody to run them and the sound? We figure we could handle 'em fer ya."

Had she heard them right? Sugar sat up straighter and looked from one man to the other. Applegate yanked on his waistband and then stood with his thin shoulders back, his thumbs hooked through his belt loops. Stanley ran a hand over his thinning hair and rocked back on his heels. Both men were nodding.

"But—"

Applegate waved a hand. "Now, Sugar, 'but' ain't what we come ta hear you say. We're stinkin' bored ta death."

"This re-tarment's about ta kill us," Stanley snapped. "We thank this'll work, and we know we kin do the job. Sounds kinda fun."

Their offer touched her. And really, what did she have

to lose? She rose slowly. They wanted to help and she needed all of that she could get. She'd worry about their technical "know-how" later. "I can't pay much. And the hours are going to be long some days and sporadic on others."

Applegate's bushy brows met as he looked from Stanley to her. "That means we're hired?"

Sugar nodded and prayed she wouldn't live to regret this. But there was no way she could turn them down. "Welcome to the show, boys."

Ross was standing in front of the barn when Sugar drove up, and as he watched her bump along over the gravel road, he felt a mixture of dread and anticipation. When he wasn't disagreeing with her, he enjoyed her company. Yesterday had been no different. How could he be so leery of a person and yet so attracted to her at the same time? When he'd told her that he would help her, and she'd thrown herself into his arms, he'd almost lost his focus.

He was determined to ensure that that wouldn't happen again. This was business, and he'd do well to remember it.

"Hey, cowboy," she called as she hurried out of her car. "I've been so excited about this that I could hardly work today."

The woman's eyes were shining so brightly with joy that he couldn't help feeling charged up himself. She came to a stop in front of him, put her hands on her hips and looked up at him playfully. "Fancy meeting you here."

His mouth went dry as he stared down into those eyes. "Yeah, imagine that."

"Hey, I have news."

"You do? What's that?" he asked, turning toward the barn so they would break eye contact.

"Applegate and Stanley offered to work lights and sound."

That drew his gaze right back to her face. "What did you say?"

"I said yes. I think it will work out well. Haley already told me she was worried that her granddad was bored. So this will be good for him and Stanley. They were so excited."

"Well, great. I know they can do it. They might be old, but they're both sharp as tacks. Like my grandpop. He worked right up until he passed away."

"With you right there beside him, I bet. Just like you will be with Applegate and Stanley."

Ross had thought of his grandpop a lot since his talk with the preacher. Once again, he contemplated the barn to avoid eye contact. "He'd really like that I'm helping you do this." Ross knew it was true. "I couldn't stop thinking about it last night."

"I'm glad, because I couldn't, either. You cannot imagine how happy you've made me. I was so full of ideas last night. I mean, I've been poring over scripts and skits since I got here, and nothing feels right. I've been toying with a one-woman show based on some vignettes, but I'm still not positive."

"It will come." They started toward the barn and he was overcome with the strongest sense of anticipation. He glanced at Sugar and could tell that she felt it, too. He pushed the door open, and she slowly stepped across the threshold and stopped.

"Oh, Ross, it's perfect. Can't you just see it? Families are going to come here and see our show, and they're going to laugh and smile and go home happy. It is going to be fantastic."

"Yeah," he said, tearing his gaze away from her animated face to view the silent, cavernous barn. "I can remember looking out over our audience back in Branson and seeing the families sitting together having a great time. I think that my grandpop got more joy out of that than any other part of the show."

"What about you?" Sugar asked softly.

"I did, too. But like I said, for me there was always something missing. You know, for a long time, I had aspirations similar to yours."

"You did?"

He smiled at her startled expression. "Not Hollywood, but Nashville. I thought that was my ultimate destination. But that was when I was in my teenage years, before I fully understood that it wasn't what I wanted. And that I wasn't talented enough."

"Why do you say that? I loved the tone of your voice when you were singing to your tractor."

He grunted. "My cows were listening, too. They don't mind a less-than-perfect voice. But entertaining isn't all about talent. You as well as I know that there are a million talented people out there."

"Boy, do I ever," she said.

"It's like that Tim McGraw song, 'How Bad Do You Want It.' The lyrics talk about what it takes to make it in the music business. Like they say, you've got to want it so much that you're willing to sacrifice anything to get it. You've got to eat, sleep and dream it. It's got to be everything to you. I didn't have that drive. I didn't have the desire to risk my everyday happiness for something that could, but more probably wouldn't, happen. You have that, I think."

Sugar nodded and let out a long breath. "I've always had such tunnel vision when it comes to becoming a star that the idea of not making it scares me silly. I just can't think about it. I've lived, breathed, dreamed it for so long…"

He smiled at her, knowing it was true.

"Hey," she said, her jaw jutting. "If that's pity, then zip it. I love what I'm doing and where I'm going. I will make it. I will."

He didn't doubt it. "It's not pity. Believe it or not, I admire your drive. And I do want to help you. I've got the background, and you were right when you said I shouldn't waste it."

"You shouldn't. God gave it to you for a reason."

Seeing her smiling up at him so sincerely, he knew this was what he was supposed to do.

He told her about talking with Pastor Allen the day before. "He said something else that got me to thinking. He said God may have meant my background to be my preparation for now. To bring me here to help you."

She tipped her head to the side and smiled. "What do you think?"

She unnerved him, that's what he thought. The way she looked at him, the way she smiled at him. The way being around her kept him from thinking straight. "I believe he might be right." Ross didn't add that it scared him, but it did. Looking at her, he knew that she had everything to gain from this partnership, while he…he had everything to lose.

Chapter Twelve

Wow. Ross thought God had prepared him to help her? Yesterday, she'd been grateful that Ross had finally agreed to do so. But now to know that he believed God had had a hand in it...it made his decision mean so much more.

"You know we are going to fight," she said finally, half joking and half serious.

He crossed his arms across his chest. "Hey, didn't you hear? I'm the boss."

Oh, the man was so appealing! "Hey, yourself, boss man. Let's get this show on the road." She stepped farther into the barn, putting her focus back where it was supposed to be—on her dream.

He passed by her and crossed to the ladder leading to the hayloft. "This is where we'll produce the show—lights, sound. Come up." He climbed the ladder practically before she had time to blink, his boots clicking on the wooden rungs. Cowboys.

She followed him up and took his offered hand at the top. No matter how much she tried to deny it, she still felt that jolt of awareness shoot all the way to her toes the instant his strong fingers wrapped around hers. Thankfully, as soon as she was standing beside him, he let go and moved a few steps away. She studied the expanse of open space. Feeling jumpy, she walked to the edge and pointed down toward the back of the barn. "This is your domain, and there is where I see the stage. *My* domain."

"So far, so good."

"This is my plan," she said. "We're going to need lights. I'm thinking I'll rent the lighting and the sound system. I have some backing, but not enough to go out and buy something like that, at least, not at first. I was online last night and found a company that has everything I need. What do you think?"

He held up a hand. "Hold it. That's my department, remember? Let me make some calls and see what I can turn up. I still have a few connections." He gave her a half smile and she gave him one right back.

"If you think you're going to get any complaints from me on that, you are wrong. If you have any way of getting the equipment at a good rate, then I'll wish you well and sit tight. Believe me, my brain is full enough already." She stared down at the area where the stage would be. "I have all these ideas floating around in my head, but I just haven't got the entire picture yet. Not having to worry about every aspect is going to free me up so that I can concentrate."

"You'll get it."

She noted his encouraging smile and serious eyes and was struck by how good it felt to have someone to share this with her. She'd never had that before, and the very idea filled her with wonder.

"So tell me, what did you do in your family's show? Give me specifics." She was overtaken with the urge to learn all about him.

"I sang. I'm not that funny and I'm a terrible actor. So I'll sing in your show, but don't think I'm doing any acting. I'll leave that to you." He tapped her on the tip of her nose, his eyes twinkling. He seemed so at ease now that he'd made his mind up to help her.

She was suddenly aware again of how close he was. "I don't believe that you can't act."

"Believe it. No acting for me."

"I think you could be a star. We could do it together." She wasn't teasing.

"Not if I can help it. Besides, even if you could work a miracle and I was suddenly Brad Pitt, that isn't something that appeals to me."

She shook her head, clucking in disappointment. "I bet your family missed you when you left the show."

"Nope. I have some really talented cousins. Not to mention my mom and my uncles."

No way was the guy not missed. He had so much presence. "I'd love to see your family's show sometime."

He looked thoughtful for a moment before answering. "They tour a few times during the year. We get this up and running, they'll come do a show for you and the town."

"Cool! That's a great idea, Ross." Why hadn't she thought of that before? "After I'm gone, you could carry this on, book other shows. You know, mix it up a little. Really make something out of this place."

"Maybe. We'll see." Something unreadable flickered in his eyes. "After you're gone, it might not be the same."

They were both silent at that.

She wasn't sure what to make of such a statement. Was it personal? She wasn't ready to explore that. Time to change the subject. *Fast.* "So come on, let me show you what I have in mind and you can tell me what you think." She walked to the ladder and swung onto it. "We have a lot to get done in a short amount of time. So chop-chop." She clambered down the ladder.

When she looked up, he was still standing there gazing down at her. Her heart hammered at the expression in those green eyes. Attraction had been their steady companion from the moment they met, but she knew he was just as intent as she was to keep it at bay. As she stared up at him, she had to remind herself that this could not get personal.

But from the way her heart was hammering inside her chest, she knew she would have a struggle on her hands.

A little over a week later, on a Thursday morning, Sugar walked over to Sam's to grab a cup of coffee. A much-needed cup, since she'd been up most of the night working on the skits. Pushing through the heavy swinging door of the diner, she almost ran into Applegate and Stanley heading out.

"Hey, guys, what's up?" It was not quite eleven o'clock and they normally played checkers until almost noon. Even helping out with the theater hadn't interfered with their checkers playing.

The sweet old grumps had been out to the barn for the last five nights, making sure all the cowboys who'd shown up to build the benches and stage were doing things right. She'd been amazed by all the folks who had come to pitch in, and couldn't believe how quickly things were happening.

"Nothin's up," Applegate said, shooting her a look that could only be described as guilty.

"Oh, yeah?" she asked, her curiosity rising a notch.

"Does a man have to be up to somethin' jest because he's movin' around?"

"Um, no," she said. "I didn't mean it literally. I guess I meant to say good morning."

"Good mornin' ta you, too," Stanley said, then shoved Applegate past her. "Now get a move on, App, time's a wastin'."

They disappeared through the swinging door and she watch them through the window as they practically jumped into App's truck. At least Applegate did. It took Stanley three tries to get his short, plump leg raised high enough to step on the running board so he could pull himself into the vehicle.

"You here fer some of that fancy coffee you like so much?" Sam asked, coming to a halt beside her and startling her so badly she jumped.

"Yes. Now tell me, what's up with them?"

"You kidding? With those two, who knows?" the wiry man grunted and led the way to the counter.

She slid onto a stool and watched as he lifted the canister filled with a mixture of cinnamon, cocoa and sugar he'd concocted just for her. She still couldn't get over the fact that he'd done such a thing. She smiled as he dumped a spoonful into the bottom of a paper cup, filled it with coffee, then snagged a can of whipped cream out of the fridge. Looking more like a man using a fire extinguisher than a coffeehouse barista, he blasted the coffee mixture with enough topping to put out a small forest fire, then slid it her way.

It wasn't Starbucks, but Sugar had gotten used to Sam's equivalent. That he tried so hard to give her what she wanted touched her. And really, the mixture he'd come up with was delicious, with just enough cinnamon and cocoa to satisfy her taste buds. Who'd have thunk it?

"Still don't know why you want ta mess up a good cup of coffee with that concoction," Sam grumbled, watching her take a sip. "What's more unbelievable is now I got several other ladies comin' in here orderin' the same awful drank."

She grinned at him. "You should charge us four bucks a cup and you'd make a mint."

He scowled. "Them ingredients don't cost me any more'n sugar and cream, and you don't see me chargin' anybody fer *that*, do ya?"

She had a feeling the whipped cream added to the cost a bit, but he did have a point on the rest. "You're a real sweetheart, Sam, you know that? Your Adela is a lucky woman." Sugar hopped off the stool. "I'll catch you later. And thanks for this."

"Anytime. And it's me who's the lucky one when it comes to my Adela. All the whipped cream in the world don't even begin to compare to that sweet little lady."

Sugar was feeling happy as she left. True love was such a nice thing to see, and when Sam and Adela looked at each other, it was evident that they truly had something special.

Heading out the door, Sugar marveled at how her perception of Mule Hollow had changed over the last couple of weeks. The people, the town, even the wall-to-wall wood of the diner had grown on her since her first day. She still couldn't see spending her whole life in a place this small, but she could understand its appeal.

"Load up," Haley said, meeting her on the sidewalk in front of the office. "I need your opinion on a couple of color schemes before the painters come."

"You're the boss." Sipping her coffee, Sugar climbed into Haley's car. Her friend had not only opened a real-estate office, but was also refurbishing and flipping a few properties. Slowly but surely. That was the thing about Mule Hollow real estate—it moved at a snail's pace compared to the L.A. market. Haley didn't seem to mind, though. It had been a total surprise to Sugar how much her friend enjoyed decorating. She'd invited her to get involved in a flip, but Sugar didn't have the extra time or the desire.

"Haley, I have to be honest with you. I totally couldn't understand you giving up your career in Beverly Hills real estate to come out here and do this." She looked around the place that she'd first seen in Haley's e-mailed pictures a few months before. "This is wonderful, though. I sort of get it now. For you, not me."

Haley laughed. "'Sort of' is better than you telling me I was stark raving mad like you did for so long."

Sugar looked sheepish. "I was a little brittle, wasn't I?"

"Were you ever—but I always thought that once you came out here, met Will and saw what I was doing, you'd see the light. By the way, are we still on for dinner Saturday night?"

Sugar studied the paint chips Haley had given her. Haley and Will had invited her and Ross to dinner at their house. "Sure are. But, Haley, I hope you aren't getting any ideas. I mean, Ross and I are working okay together. But…"

"You know you like him."

"I'm not going to deny it. The man is…likable. But we have an understanding."

"And what's that?"

"We both understand that we are nothing more than business partners. Anything personal would be a mistake. You know that's true."

Haley pouted. "I don't like it. I want you to fall in love and stay here. He's perfect for you."

Sugar rolled her eyes, not about to let her friend know exactly how attracted she was to Ross. "That won't happen, so stop."

"But you have to admit that the man is really bending over backward to make your dream come true. You can't tell me he's going to all this trouble just because he thinks it's the right thing to do."

"Yes, I can. Partly. And the other part…well, he doesn't know it, but deep down, he wants to do it."

"For you?"

"No, silly. For himself. You should see him when he talks about working with his grandpop. His eyes sparkle. There's still a connection there and I think he really misses it. He just won't admit it. I haven't gotten it totally figured out. But I'm going to."

Haley didn't say anything, just smiled.

"Stop that," Sugar said. "Stop thinking whatever it is you're thinking." Haley could hope and even pray, but Sugar was not going to fall in love with Ross, get married and live happily ever after in Mule Hollow, Texas. It wasn't going to happen. She wouldn't let it. No matter how much she'd come to treasure the time spent working beside him.

This was business, and when the time came, she would be out of here. She'd not given anyone any reason to expect any differently. She'd made no promises that would bind her in any way, and that was how it would remain.

"Besides, Haley," she said as they left the house, colors chosen. "There is still so much to do before we are anywhere near ready for a show. Do you realize," she said as they climbed back into the car, "opening night is scheduled for the third weekend of August? I'm not near prepared. Not only do I not have my skits totally figured out, but I have no lights or sound system. Ross said he'd take care of it, but it's been a week, and so far, nothing. When I ask him about them, he just tells me not to worry."

Haley laughed. "It's only *been* a week. Relax. I'm sure he's got it under control."

Sugar hoped so. She'd been practicing her skits every spare moment that she didn't spend hunting for a play that she'd like better. She was trying to make sure she was ready with at least the skits if that was all she ended up with.

"Besides, I'm getting antsy. I'm ready to practice on the stage with lights and costumes. And a cast!"

Haley chuckled. "Sugar, you are going to get an ulcer if you keep this up. Think about everything you *do* have lined up, not what you don't. You've got the tryouts coming up and since the guys know what's expected this time, they're on board and ready. Norma Sue, Esther Mae and Adela are heading up a blitz of a promo drive. Not to mention Molly talking you up in her column. Gracious, Sugar, that's a lot."

Haley was right. The ladies were planning to drive the seventy miles to the closest sizeable town to begin handing out flyers about the show. They were the self-appointed advertisement committee, and she knew they would get the job done. The community was already buzzing, since Molly had mentioned the show in her newspaper column. It was all just like Sugar had hoped. Everything was poised to attract some media attention, and maybe some reviewers other than Molly. After all the obstacles when she'd first arrived, Sugar had to calm down and remember that things were going smoothly now.

"I want your opinion on another place," Haley said as she passed through town, heading out in the direction of the barn.

"Sure thing, boss lady," Sugar said. "But I didn't know you were working on a house out here."

"Oh, well, you know."

Sugar glanced at her friend. "Are you hedging about something?"

"Hedging? Me? No."

They got to the barn and Haley turned into the drive. "But since we're here, I want to look at something."

Something was up. Applegate and Stanley were there, and so was Ross. And Will's truck, also. Sugar frowned at Haley, who was exiting the vehicle as if it was on fire.

Sugar wasn't stupid, but she figured that whatever it was had to be a good surprise. The first thing she noticed as she followed Haley in was that everyone was standing up in the hayloft. Today, though, something was different. There were lights up there! And speakers!

"Surprise!" they all yelled. App hit a switch, and a light beamed down on Haley, who'd stepped onto the middle of the stage. They had a spotlight!

"Where did that come from?" she squealed, awed that they'd worked so hard to get this surprise set up. *This* was why they'd all been in such a hurry earlier, and why Haley had kept her occupied.

Ross walked to the edge of the loft and smiled. "My family has to upgrade their show sometimes. They scrounged around for some things they'd outgrown, and donated them to the cause."

Sugar blinked hard. Swallowed harder. "Wow," she managed to croak.

"Well, don't jest stand thar," Applegate roared. "Get yorself up here and take a look. Thar's more buttons on these here boards than I ever saw in all my born days."

Ross was grinning as she grabbed the rung of the ladder and started climbing toward him. He'd come through for her again. She smiled at him as she stepped onto the platform. "Once again, you are my real-life hero," she said, breathless with excitement.

"All in a day's work for a hero, ma'am."

On impulse, she brushed a kiss across his cheek, then hurried to look at the control panel and the light setup.

Will was standing beside Stanley. "You must have helped install all of those," she stated.

He nodded. "That I did. I'm glad I was able to contribute something to the show."

"Oh, it's all grand." She ran her hand over the light board and couldn't believe that it was there, sitting beside a soundboard. She looked at Ross. "I guess they just happened to outgrow this, too?" She scanned the barn, taking in all the speakers.

"They've been in business for a lot of years. You should see the back room of that theater. What they didn't have, my dad got from some of his other friends. But there was one request."

"What?"

"They do want to come up one weekend during their off-season, and do a show here. Nothing huge, only part of the cast. We just have to schedule it, and we've got a date."

Sugar was speechless, but only for a second. "Oh, Ross. That will garner some great publicity for the theater!"

"Yup, ain't that somethin," Applegate said. "We might could become the next little Nashville!"

Haley laughed from down below. "That might be stretching it, Granddad, but it is a great opportunity."

Everyone started talking at once. Sugar felt like she needed a chair. Thank goodness there was one near. She pulled it out and sank into it. "I'm in business," she said, her voice cracking. "I'm really, really in business."

"Looks that way," Ross said, his expression one she could only describe as boyish satisfaction.

Thank you, she mouthed.

A wide, goofy smile spread across his handsome face. She knew it was in response to the matching one spreading across hers.

Chapter Thirteen

"Be the hero of my show."

"No, Sugar." Ross stared at the hardheaded woman in front of him and fought to hold his ground against her persuasive smile. "We've been through this. I don't want to be on stage other than to sing a few songs."

It was just the two of them in the barn now. He'd offered to give her a ride back to town, since Haley had suspiciously decided she wanted to follow her husband home. App and Stanley had run off, too, leaving Ross alone with Sugar. It was a position he'd been trying to avoid. Until now, he'd succeeded most of the times they'd spent working on the benches and the stage. He didn't want to admit that he was afraid of being alone with her, but he knew he was. He'd been attracted to the woman from day one. A smart defense against letting his attraction for her grow was a strong offense.

He needed to keep his distance in order to maintain his perspective.

But knowing how anxious Sugar had been to get sound equipment and lights had messed him up. He had figured she would want to spend time checking it out, so he'd agreed to stay with her instead of taking her back to town as soon as everyone else abandoned them.

Looking at her now, at the persuasive glint in her eyes, he had to remind himself to shake his head and hold his own. They'd been getting along so well during the construction period, but she still had to get it through her pretty little head that he was *not* going to be the hero of her show. No way.

True, he couldn't get over how much he was enjoying getting this show up and running. If someone had asked him a month ago if he'd ever go back into the entertainment business, he'd have said no. In fact he *had* said no. Several times. Funny thing was, he'd never felt as satisfied by the business as he had once he'd started building the stage. And seeing the light shining in Sugar's eyes.

He pushed that counterproductive thought out of his head and gave her an extra-stern stare. "We had a deal. I help with the production and sing a couple of songs. That's it."

He was sitting on the edge of the stage now, determined not to be manipulated into doing something he would regret. Not an easy task when the woman was staring at him as if he was the best thing since those gumdrops she loved to eat.

"No," he said again when she batted her beautiful eyes at him and smiled sweetly. "And stop looking at me like that."

"I'm looking at you with complete adulation because you are a surprising man, Ross Denton," she said, coming toward him down the center aisle. She waved her arm to encompass the rows of benches that he and his friends had built. "You did all of this. And now the sound system. And your family…"

She had momentarily veered off course to pat him on the back, but he knew she hadn't given up on casting him as her costar. She didn't give up on anything. He clenched his jaw, determined not to be moved.

Determined not to give in.

She stopped at the front row and studied him. She had on jeans and boots and a red tank top with a star on the front. That star reminded him that her heart was in Hollywood. Ross would be a fool if he let himself forget that.

Fool or not, he struggled against the sudden urge to put his arms around her and agree to anything she asked of him. *Oh, no you don't. Back it up there, bud.*

That was harder still because he'd truly enjoyed being with her over the last two weeks. The connection he felt to his grandpop had grown as he'd worked on the production. Now he knew the exhilaration his grandparents had felt as they'd built their show up from nothing but a barn and their talent. He owed that feeling to the woman in front of him, and that was another complication, making it harder to listen to the bells of alarm clanging somewhere deep inside of him.

"Thank you for doing so much for me." She stepped closer.

"It's what I agreed to do."

"So are you going to finally sing for me? Me, not your tractor or your cows."

He laughed. He should have known this was coming. The woman was a persistent bombshell. "I'll sing. That was part of the deal." He raised an eyebrow to make his point—that he was fulfilling everything he'd promised. She chuckled, and the sound rippled through him like music. He walked away from it, moving toward the sound booth, and put a good ten feet between them before he turned and asked, "So what do you want me to sing?" His blamed voice sounded like gravel. He'd wanted to kiss her. It wasn't the first time the thought had crossed his mind.

"That same song you were singing the day I found out your secret. The one about God's love and a father's love being unending. Sing that one. I'm thinking it may be one to use for the show. Of course, we'd need to get permission if we use it, which is something else I need to take care of."

"It'll all get done. I can take care of most of that. But you know I haven't sung to anyone but my cows in a long time."

She tucked a stray strand of hair behind her ear, her hand lingering there. "Then I think it's high time you primed those pipes, don't you? And we really need to make sure all this new equipment works, so chop-chop."

"Yes, ma'am. Just for you then."

"Now that's what I'm talking about—a man who knows how to keep a smile on a girl's face."

His eyes were immediately drawn to her smiling lips,

and he almost groaned. "Um, I'll go turn on the system. Hang on." He shot toward the loft like a man running from a burning building. Grabbing the ladder, he climbed up the rungs, then stomped over to the black soundboard. As a kid, this board had fascinated him. At the moment, it held no interest at all. Every fiber of his being was fighting a fascination for the woman that stood below him in front of the small stage. *Focus, man,* he willed himself. Focus.

He got the microphone set, took a few deep breaths and then went to sing to Sugar. Thank goodness she'd asked for a song about God's love and not a romantic one. He'd have been completely undone if she'd asked him to sing something like "When a Man Loves a Woman." Not that he loved her. It would have just been awkward. Yeah, awkward. That was exactly what it would be.

She was sitting on the edge of the stage when he walked up, mike in hand. "You know, this would be better with music," he stated. "Helps hide the imperfections."

"Would you stop already? I know you can sing, so quit being so bashful."

He chuckled and lifted the mike. "Well, here goes nothing."

Nothing my foot! Sugar thought as Ross started singing. She felt as if his rich, melodic voice was embracing her. The man could protest all he wanted to, but he was so talented she was jealous. In a good way.

But it was more than that. Just as she'd suspected, when he turned toward the spotlight, his fabulous, intense eyes caught the light and reflected it. And when he sang, he made her believe and feel every word. He had a gift, and she was certain every person in the audience would feel it and see it.

By the time he'd finished the song, she wasn't smiling any longer. She was sitting silent and awed.

This man should be on the radio.

That was all she could think. What would he sound like with music and studio effects behind him?

He lowered the mike and gave a half grin, just a quirk of one side of his mouth, as if to say, "And that's it, nothing much."

Nothing much? She had chill bumps on her arms. Looking up at him, she said the first thing that came to mind. "You've got some lucky cows."

He chuckled. "That's a matter of opinion."

"Goodness, Ross, what were you thinking? You *belong* on that stage!"

He looked less than impressed with her gushing. "Speaking of stage, fair is fair," he drawled. "Hop up here and give me a little show. I know you've been practicing, and I know official rehearsals are about to start, but I want a sneak peek."

Sugar's stomach dropped, and—for the first time in her life, she felt self-conscious. But she was more than ready to actually work on that stage. And she really needed something to take her mind off Ross. She just wasn't sure what he would think of her program. It was original material, and not at all what she'd ever thought she would be doing.

He was watching her with an encouraging expression, so she drew a deep breath. "Okay, here's what I've been working on. Remember, it's original stuff, written by me." She made a face. "And it's not at all what I was planning when I first got to town…. It's a couple of fish-out-of-water scenarios."

She hopped from her seat and moved toward the stage, still yakking away and feeling as if she'd rather crawl in a hole than perform. "I just started writing one night about me coming to Mule Hollow. You know, how differently I looked at things. And since it had to be mostly me doing the acting…well, I started this piece. I'm not totally happy with it, but I think it might work."

"Sugar…"

She stopped talking and looked at him. She felt queasy and her palms were clammy.

"Stop talking and do it. I'm sure it'll be great."

She took another breath, swallowed to try and wet her suddenly dry throat, and nodded. "Right. Okay, here goes. You sit over there."

"Are you kidding? I'm going up top to work the spot-light."

She laughed and shoved her fear aside. "Then get up there, mister," she said, forcing herself to sound in control. "After all, a star is about to be born…after you, of course. I think you're going to sing one song and steal the show."

He grunted and climbed back to the loft. Outside, the sun had gone down. As he adjusted the lights, Sugar's nervousness calmed, replaced with pure adrenaline. This was a feeling she knew, loved and lived for. She gazed out over the shadowy rows of benches and then up to where Ross sat. Because of the bright lights, she could no longer see him. It was as if she was in her own little world. A world she loved.

She inhaled slowly, then exhaled, releasing all extraneous thoughts. She closed her eyes and called up the words she'd written, felt the emotions captured in them as she inhaled once more, seeking that special zone.

Then she opened her eyes and started doing what she was born to do....

She blew him away! The woman was as good as anybody he'd ever seen! She was funny, totally mesmerizing...and he hated her show with all his heart. But it had nothing to do with her ability.

Ross just stood there when she'd finished, his insides all twisted up with conflicting emotions. He couldn't move. Sugar's one-woman monologue about coming to small-town America and leaving civilization behind would probably be a big success. But it lacked something. She was better than her show, that was for certain. Then again, it could be that he just didn't liked the story. The scenes said, loud and clear, what Sugar made no secret of, herself: she was not a small-town girl.

The three scenes she did for him showcased with great finesse the shock and horror of a city girl gone country. She displayed a terrific combination of comedic timing and pure, awesome stage presence. Despite his discontent with her message, he even laughed. It was impossible not to. With some fine-tuning, she would have a hit on her hands. Still, every scene showed him he had no business getting any ideas about her staying around. And no matter how he denied it, he knew that this was what was eating at him. That was why he hated the show. It was for personal reasons…and that was not good. Not good at all.

"So, what do you think?" she called after her "Tango with the Beavers" skit.

He swallowed hard. "You're talented, Sugar Rae. Very talented." He could hear the less-than-thrilled tone in his voice and was afraid she'd heard it, too. He turned away from her to cover the equipment with a drop cloth, not wanting her to see his dismay. She'd be leaving as soon as she could. And he was helping her do it. Hollywood was crazy for not recognizing the beauty and talent in this woman.

He climbed down the ladder with feet of lead. She was waiting for him at the bottom, staring toward the darkened stage. He fought the urge to drape an arm over her shoulders and hug her when she looked up at him, her expression full of wonder.

"That was amazing. I almost felt like I did when I used to dress up for my grandmothers and put on a show with nothing more than a cardboard box as a prop. Before I became so obsessed with making it. It felt natural and free…and fabulous."

She was fabulous. He hooked his thumbs onto his belt and held on so he wouldn't reach for her. "I know what you mean," he said, feeling as close to her in that moment as he'd ever felt to anyone. "That's what I felt when I was first singing on my grandpop's knee. I lost that feeling somewhere along the way." He looked at the dark stage. "But I felt it again tonight, singing for you and then watching you perform," he admitted. "I'd forgotten how much I once enjoyed it." It was true. Even if her skits bothered him, he'd felt that satisfaction surge through him, watching her and singing to her.

"Then be my hero. If you'd be my hero, I know I could come up with the rest of the show. We'd be great together."

"No." No way! "You just don't quit, do you?"

"No. I think the show still needs something. I like the skits but that's just a warm-up. It doesn't feel like a real *show*. I still have to come up with something that involves the cowboys. And I need one particular cowboy to be the glue."

"The glue?"

"Yes. I think I want to do a romance. Since that's the kind of movie I want to star in, it's only logical."

Romance? "Nope. I'm sticking to my guns here, Sugar. Count me out."

She propped her hands on her waist and cocked a hip as she considered him.

"Stop it right now," Ross exclaimed. "I can see that mind of yours trying to figure out a way to get me to do what you want me to." The little minx never stopped trying to get the upper hand. "It's not going to happen." There was no way in the universe he was going to play her *love* interest up on that stage!

No. Way.

Chapter Fourteen

Sugar slammed the file drawer closed and swung around just as Haley came into the office.

"Hey, what's with the scowl? Is something wrong?" Haley asked, dropping her purse on her desk and herself in her chair.

"You could say so. I need Ross to be the leading man in my show, and he won't budge. Won't even talk about it." Sugar clapped her palm to her forehead. "The dude acts like I'm asking him to stand up there and play Romeo for me. I don't get him."

"Sugar, the man has agreed to help you with the production *and* sing for you. He told you in the beginning he didn't want to act."

"And I'm grateful for his help. But I need something special for this show. I did my skits last night, and felt so at home and inspired on the stage, but I *know* I need something more for it to stand out. My heart is telling me that Ross is that something. He's special."

Haley looked troubled, but didn't say anything. "What?" Sugar asked.

"You know I love you. You're my friend, but…well, listen to yourself. That entire statement was all about you. I don't think I've ever heard the word *I* used so many times."

Sugar stared at her friend. That wasn't fair. "I won't apologize for going for what I think I need to get me what I want. The whole reason for the production is to draw some notice. If I don't shoot for the best, then I'm just spinning my wheels. And Ross Denton is the best. The man makes a statement just by stepping into a room. On stage, he will translate into pure magic. I know it."

"Okay, wildcat. Calm down." Haley lifted a hand in surrender. "I get what you're saying. And all *I* can say is, the poor guy might as well give in now. One thing is for certain, dinner promises to be interesting tomorrow night. Did you remember?"

Sugar gaped. "Oh, I forgot! We didn't talk all the way into town last night." She nibbled the inside of her lip. "I was so frustrated that I didn't even think about tomorrow night." She'd been too dazed. "I have no clue if we're still on or not."

"Sure you are. I'm not accepting any excuses. Will has his thickest steaks marinating as we speak, and he is an excellent griller. You two are working together—you just have to get past this, and move forward. Dinner with us will help with that, and then rehearsals will start and things will be fine. Right?"

Sugar wasn't so sure things would be fine…but if she

wanted to make this show work, then she needed to get past this, and quickly. "You're right," she said, snatching up the phone book and flipping through it until she found Ross's phone number. Then she grabbed the phone and dialed.

"Who are you calling?" Haley asked, noting the gleam in her eyes.

"My date." She motioned for her friend to stay quiet as he picked up. "Hello, Ross, this is Sugar."

"Hello." His surprise rang through the phone line loud and clear.

"I called because I wasn't certain you remembered we were supposed to go to Haley's tomorrow night."

"I remembered."

He didn't sound at all pleased about it.

"Would you like me to meet you there?"

"Sugar, I'll pick you up at seven. There's no need for both of us to drive all the way out to Will and Haley's. Especially since you're on my way."

"Well, fine. Since you put it that way, how could a girl refuse?" She slammed the phone down and glared at Haley, who was smiling. "Don't say anything."

Haley didn't. She chuckled instead.

Sugar wore her favorite sundress, and had just finished brushing her hair when Ross knocked on her door. She'd begun to feel a little bad for giving him so much grief about being her hero. Maybe she *was* being selfish. She took one last glimpse in the mirror and told herself to behave. Then she went to the door and swept it open.

Ross was holding his hat in his hands and looked every bit the hero.

"Hi," he said. "Are you ready?"

"No. Um, before we go, I need to say that I'm sorry for the way I've been harassing you about acting in my show. I'll stop. Haley told me I was being selfish."

He raised a brow. Sugar wondered if he'd practiced it as she had or if he'd been born with the talent. She was going to have to ask him sometime…but not now. "Maybe I was," she added, when he didn't say anything.

"I think I'm beginning to understand why your agent keeps you away from producers' doorsteps."

To her surprise, Ross smiled—which made Sugar smile. "I know I can be a bit of a pain. I promise to behave tonight. I've given myself a stern talking-to in my bathroom mirror and I have sworn that I will be nice to you."

"So I guess I can count my blessings this evening, but watch out on the other days?"

She shot him a smile and deliberately didn't reply as she headed down the stairs.

Despite her apology, Ross was not very talkative as they drove the fifteen miles out to Haley's. "So what did you do today?" she asked. "Play with my little ninja buddies?"

"No time to play with them today. I played cowboy instead."

She studied his profile. "I haven't seen you on a horse…matter of fact, I haven't seen but one guy actually on a horse since I got to town. And he was off in the distance."

Ross chuckled. The sound rumbled through her in the most pleasant way.

"You haven't exactly been out and about all that much. You're usually either at work or at the barn. From what I've observed, you aren't doing anything that doesn't have to do with this production."

"I've been to Sam's and to church, but there are only so many hours in the day. If I want to get this done then that's what I have to do."

"Is this how you lived back in Hollywood?"

She shrugged. "Basically. I worked part-time as Haley's assistant, went to auditions, and had acting class at night. I loved it. I would have loved it more if something had ever come of it. But still, I enjoyed every minute."

"What did you do for fun?"

"That *was* fun."

"I admire your drive and determination, but I'm beginning to wonder about the balance in your life."

Sugar had heard that before. Members of her family had made the same point many times. "Look, don't worry about me and balance. You sound like my folks and my brothers. I may be a little driven, but this is just the way I am. I don't know any other way to be."

He didn't say anything else as he drove through the beautiful entrance to Will and Haley's property. Sugar studied the intricate iron gate and tried not to let Ross's words get to her. "Will is very talented, isn't he?"

"That's for certain. He stays busy, too, gets orders from all over the place for his work." As Ross pulled to a halt, Haley came out of the house, waving. Sugar was relieved to get out of the truck. She didn't like being judged by him.

The next couple of hours were fun. It was more than evident that Haley and Will were happy. Watching them together put to rest any and all lingering reservations Sugar had about her friend moving back here.

After they'd eaten, Will took them out to his workshop, and surprised her with a sign he'd made for the theater.

"Oh, Will, I can't believe you made this for me. It's perfect." She'd named the theater simply The Barn Theater, and Will had crafted a replica of Ross's barn below the name. He'd used his welding torch to create something simple but perfect in beautiful black iron.

She looked at Ross. He seemed as touched by the gift as she was. She hugged Will, then Haley. "Thank you both for everything you've done. It all means so much to me. But this…this is outstanding."

"We'll hang it tomorrow," Ross said, and Will agreed.

Later, as they rode home, he was quiet again.

"I just can't believe Will did that. It is simply amazing. He's really a great guy. You know, I tried to get Haley to move back to L.A. I mean, I thought she'd lost her mind when she gave everything up for him…but did you see them together? It's like they really belong together."

"What about you, Sugar? Are you looking for love?"

She studied Ross's face, illuminated by the low light from the dashboard. "One day. Not now."

"Not until you're famous," he finished for her.

"That's right." She felt defensive for some reason.

Maybe it was the glance he slid her way. "There isn't anything wrong with that."

"I didn't say there was."

"Then why did you look at me that way?"

"Because I can't stop thinking about what we were talking about earlier tonight. Have you ever had any kind of life that wasn't focused on attaining your dream?"

What was his problem? "Why are you suddenly obsessing about my life?"

"I'm just wondering why all your experiences are wrapped up in this goal of yours. It isn't healthy. You need something to balance the one-sided life you've built for yourself."

They had reached her apartment, but she didn't get out. Who did he think he was to judge her life? "I'm single-minded."

"And *not* well-rounded."

"And what is that to you? I asked you to get involved with my show. I didn't ask you to tell me how unhealthy my life is. I have enough family who do that already, thank you very much."

Her heart was pumping and her palms were damp. It was the same feeling she got when that hideous voice started telling her to forget her dream. So what if she had no idea what she would do if she didn't make it? So what if, other than her family and Haley, she'd never taken the time to make many friends, or pursue other interests? So what if just thinking about failure made her feel lost? It was all more fuel to make her achieve her dream.

"So you think finding a husband will make my life

suddenly have meaning? That a little romance will make me a more rounded, healthier person?"

"Look, Sugar, forget what I said. I was just worrying about you. Is that so bad? You're closed off from everything but this dream. I look at you sometimes and I still see that lonely little girl stuck on that couch, with nothing but her fantasies, because she can't get up and live her own life."

Sugar swung the truck door open and bolted out. "Don't bother," she growled when he started to open his door.

"Good night, Sugar," he said, looking straight ahead.

Ooh! She slammed the door and stalked up the stairs. When she reached the top step she turned and watched his taillights disappear into the night. She was glad to see him go. The man obviously lived to push her buttons, and he was wrong about her life. He *was*.

Ross might have been wrong, but she couldn't sleep as his words kept plaguing her. He'd implied that she was afraid—*scared* to lay her dream down. The fact that he had somehow guessed at the very thought that had been bothering her for months didn't really settle well with her. She flopped over, stared up at the moonlight reflected on the ceiling, and groaned. So *what* if she failed? The very question made her queasy. "Lord," she whispered, squeezing her eyes shut. "If this isn't what you have planned for me, then what is? What?"

It was a question she'd never asked God before. And doing so now she felt exposed…and scared.

Chapter Fifteen

Sugar was late to church the next morning. She just couldn't seem to get her act together. By the time she walked into the singles class, the room was packed and the only empty chair was beside Stacy. Sugar ran through everything she knew about the woman. Stacy worked across the street from the real-estate office, at the candy store, and lived at the women's shelter Dottie and Sheriff Brady had established at their ranch. She'd come over with the other ladies the day Sugar arrived in town, but she'd held back and barely spoken. She didn't say anything now, either, just smiled when Sugar whispered, "Good morning."

Sugar took the lesson Sheriff Brady, the teacher, handed her, then cast a glance around the room. Ross wasn't there. He also wasn't at the main worship service forty-five minutes later, she discovered. She couldn't help wondering why.

When church was over, she turned down all invitations

for lunch and headed home instead. She wasn't in the mood to be around anyone. What she really wanted was to go out to the barn and see if Will and Ross were hanging the sign. But she didn't go. Oh, no. She couldn't get the thought out of her head that Ross might have missed church because he was aggravated at her. She wanted to believe it was something else that had kept him away. As he said, ranching was sometimes a seven-days-a-week job. In the end she decided that maybe she and he both needed a bit of space. A little breathing room.

So instead of going to the barn, she plopped herself on the couch in her apartment and read scripts until her eyeballs wanted to roll over and play dead.

Bedtime couldn't come soon enough!

There were just some days that were nice to say good-night to. This was the mother of all of those days. She could only hope she woke in a better mood, for everyone's sake.

Much to her surprise, she fell asleep almost the instant her head touched the pillow. But even more surprising was that she dreamed.

Sugar wasn't normally much of a dreamer. She'd always joked that since she did so much dreaming during the day, God had decided she needed the night for uninterrupted sleeping. When she wasn't stressed out, she normally slept like a rock, flat on her face. Because of it, she guessed she was going to be wrinkled as a shriveled fig before she turned fifty if she didn't figure out a way to make herself sleep on her back.

When she woke Monday morning before daybreak,

sprawled on her back, she was shocked—and she wasn't thinking about wrinkles. She was thinking about the dream she'd had. It was a good dream!

A *funny* dream.

It was about a gal moving to this wacky town and falling in love with a singing cowboy! It was a perfect girl-next-door romantic comedy, and she was the perfect actress to play it. Not that the girl was really her—no way. She had not fallen in love with Ross Denton. But still, the story line *was* similar to what had been going on between them. During the dream, the skits she'd been working on finally came into play as a whole, and she *got* it. Got that they weren't separate vignettes, but scenes of the play she'd been searching for! It was suddenly clear as day how all the bits worked together, and she wondered why she hadn't seen it before.

Sugar had never in her life had the urge to write— except for those skits, which she'd labored over with major effort—but now she felt inspired. This was *her show* and she knew it. And she *had* to get it on paper. She woke wide-eyed, with all of this clanging in her head, and hurled herself out of bed like a madwoman, hitting the bathroom at a dead run. She brushed her teeth, yanked her hair back into a ponytail, stumbled, jerked and jumped into her clothes in no time at all, then descended the stairs in a sprint. It was five-thirty in the morning when she bounded into her office chair and switched on her computer.

She'd never had this feeling before—there was no fuzziness about it. She had a full-blown story rolling in her head and raring to get out. It didn't matter that she didn't exactly know the protocol for script writing—she just started typing.

She watched in wonder as her fingers flew across the keys. As easy as turning on the faucet and letting water run, the words flowed onto the screen.

It was the absolute coolest thing that had ever happened to her. The dream burst into life like a movie. And even though she certainly *wasn't* living the romance, she knew that the tension between her and Ross was driving this emotion. Clearly, it had taken hold of her brain and done a number on her. God was good. She watched with amazement and gratitude as her show materialized before her eyes.

When Haley walked into the office at ten, Sugar was waiting, a silly grin on her face and a stack of papers primed and ready. It needed some fine-tuning, but it was done.

"Sit," Sugar said, jumping up and grabbing the pages from the printer.

"What's going on?"

"Good stuff. Wonderful stuff. You know how I've been hemming and hawing about what I was going to do? Well, I have it." She slapped the pages on the desk in front of Haley. "Read this and tell me what you think of my play."

Haley's eyes widened. "You wrote this?"

"Yeah, I did." Sugar beamed. She felt as if her chest were going to explode. "It's rough, I know, but see what you think. It just came. Like an explosion, it was full-blown in my head when I woke up this morning."

Haley picked up the stack of pages and leaned back in her chair. "This is going to be interesting."

Still awed, but suddenly exhausted from the experience, Sugar crossed to her desk and collapsed like a dishrag into her seat. What a rush that had been! She snagged a pencil and chewed on it, waiting for Haley's reaction.

She didn't have to wait long. Within seconds, her friend chuckled.

Sugar smiled. That was good.

Another chuckle erupted a few seconds later.

Then she snorted—*snorted*. Then chuckled again.

Sugar started grinning. That was all she needed. So what if the script was rough. It was getting the response she wanted, and Sugar knew she could bring it to life on the stage. All she had to do was get Ross to agree to be her hero. Oh yeah, she was ready for the fireworks to break out, but he had to take the part. There just wasn't any getting around it. This role was his.

Sure, he had a problem with acting, but he'd come through for her every other time…after a fight. He really was her living, breathing, true-life hero, and she could only hope that once he read this he would change his mind.

All she had to do was get him to read it.

"No. We've been through this, Sugar."

Ross had known he was in for trouble the moment Sugar burst into the barn. He'd been talking with Applegate and Stanley, and the old coots were now having a good ole time watching the showdown.

"Yes, we have," Sugar huffed. "And I don't mind telling you that I had an absolute horrible day yesterday thanks to you, buster. Our little conversation did quite a number on me. But you know what? I admitted that I am scared. I have no life other than this, and it's going to be pretty depressing if I fail. So, yes, I don't know what's going to happen with my life. But guess what? I want to be an actress, and if I fail, I'm going to do it knowing I gave it my all. We're dealing with a lot of things right now, me and the Lord. Things I've been needing to deal with, and that's partly because you made me so mad. So thanks," she said. "Really."

Once again, she'd said the unexpected, and Ross found himself floundering.

She waggled the pages she was still holding out to him. "Please read this. If I'm not meant to be an actress, then I'll accept that, when I have to," she said softly. "But I'm not giving up without a fight and I *need* you to play the love interest in my show. I know I'm asking a lot and that it could take time away from your ranching, but I'll help you work the cows myself if I have to in order to get your help."

"Sugar, I'm trying to give you everything I've got, but I'm telling you I am not a good actor. In my family's show, I sang. That was my talent. And, yes, sometimes I played straight man to our comedian, but that only worked because I couldn't act worth a flip, and it was funny. Don't you get it?"

"Actually, I do." She waggled the papers again. "Please, just look at it. And then tell me no if that's what you feel."

He'd spent all Sunday in search of a missing calf, and it had given him a lot of time to think about Sugar. He'd been out of line in their last conversation, and that had been eating at him. Despite his efforts, he cared about her. Taking this part wasn't going to help him fight his feelings. But she'd obviously just faced some difficult issues because he'd come down so hard on her, and it couldn't hurt to read it, right? It wasn't as if he'd actually take the part. He couldn't act well enough to play any kind of lead.

"C'mon on, son," Applegate boomed. "Least ya kin do is read the thang."

"Yep," Stanley added, just as loud. "If Sugar is willin' ta fail 'cause you ain't no good, then I'd thank you ought'n ta not be afraid ta give it a try."

Sugar smiled, and her eyes shone with sincerity. "If this is about embarrassing yourself on stage, you don't have to worry about that. I promise I will make you look good." She waggled the script again.

She could make anyone look good. Ross stared down at his boots and blew out a frustrated breath, then held out his hand. "I'll read it."

Her smile blasted to high beam as she stuffed the pages into his outstretched hand. "I *promise* you're going to like it."

Full of dread, he sat on the edge of the stage. She didn't move, and he glanced up, expecting to see a smug expression on her face. He was surprised to find that she looked almost vulnerable standing there watching him. More intrigued than he would admit, he kept his mouth shut and started reading.

He didn't get past page one when he realized she was writing about him. At least, he was pretty sure it was him. It took every ounce of control not to look up and ask her point-blank if he was this "singing cowboy."

But he didn't have to ask. She'd nailed him. Every line was something he would say—or *had* said to her.

The other thing was, it was funny. Not just funny, but fun.

By the time he had finished reading, she'd sunk onto the bench between Applegate and Stanley. They were all three frowning.

"You hated it," she said.

"Why do you say that?"

"You didn't laugh. Never even chuckled."

"Shor didn't," Applegate grunted.

Stanley nodded.

Ross had this urge to tease her, but smiled instead and let out the chuckles that he'd fought down while reading the script. "It was funny," he chuckled. "So I get the girl in the end, huh?"

Her eyes lit up. "Yes! Yes! You get the girl," she exclaimed, springing off the bench and flinging her arms around his neck in a fierce, jubilant hug.

His arms went around her automatically, holding her close. Over her shoulder, he saw App and Stanley grinning like hyenas. The old codgers knew as well as he did that he was in big trouble.

He'd just agreed to play Sugar's love interest. He was going to stand on this stage pretending to fall in love with her night after night…and frankly, it was going to be the hardest thing he'd ever done.

Aside from the fact that she was gorgeous, funny and likable, she was also a very talented actress. He was going to have to work hard to keep his wits about him. Remind himself that when he played opposite her on this stage, it was only the guy he was playing who got the girl in the end. Not *him*.

Keeping reality and fiction separate was going to be hard because he'd realized something yesterday. As he roamed his pastures looking for that lost calf, he'd accepted that he was lost, too. No matter what he told himself or how much he tried to deny it, he was falling for Sugar.

Chapter Sixteen

Ross met Sugar's dancing eyes and knew there was no way he could deny that he liked making her so happy. And if it meant taking the chance of making a fool out of himself on that stage, then so be it.

"I'm going to do this," he said firmly, "because you wrote my character as a bad actor, stilted and wooden, and that gives me freedom to goof." He couldn't help giving her a heartfelt grin. "I can't get over you writing him like that. You really have a comedic flare."

"I can't take any credit for it. It just came out like that," she said in awe. "I woke this morning with the whole thing in here." She tapped her temple. "I dreamed it, and believe me when I say I do *not* dream. Everyone talks about dreams, but it never really happened to me. Never has. If I do dream, I never remember them. So to wake up and have it there, that was an awesome experience."

The woman's face spoke volumes. Ross could watch her for hours—what was wrong with those people in Hollywood?

They held auditions on Friday night. Once word got out that a new plan had come into play the cowboy talent came out in droves. The show would be presented in four acts, with songs in between. Each cowboy was able to look at the posted song schedule, decide which show he could do, and commit to the performances that worked with his schedule.

Also, because the play revolved around Sugar and Ross, the acting parts for others were short and easily learned, which meant they could also be shifted about. With so much flexibility incorporated into the show, everyone got on board, and rehearsals began on Saturday.

By the time she arrived at the barn that night, Sugar was a ball of nerves. She'd written, rewritten, tweaked and tweaked again, and she thought she had every part of the script as ready as it could be.

Ross had worked hard getting the dressing rooms finished. Smart man that he was, he'd also built a catwalk from the loft to the backstage area, and installed a compact spiral stairway, providing quick, easy access to the loft. The man thought of everything. He amazed her.

And he was completely right when he'd said she hadn't known what she was getting herself into. There were a thousand little behind-the-scenes things that she would have had to learn by trial and error if it wasn't for him. His help on the sound and lights alone was phenomenal. Those panels with all the sliding levers and buttons still scared her every time she looked at them. But Ross patiently worked with App and Stanley, and also with Will and Bob, who'd volunteered to help take up the slack up top. They needed backup just in case feedback or glitches occurred that App and Stanley couldn't hear. The older men's hearing problems had worried Sugar when they'd asked to help, but so far, so good. And the two fellas had been so faithful in showing up. She couldn't thank them enough for all their help—especially in nudging Ross to take the part.

As the rehearsal got under way, Sugar realized that, as capable as he was, Ross seemed nervous. Though some of them wouldn't be in the show until several weeks after it opened, everyone who could had made it for the first practice, and all the guys were busy reading over their parts. She'd realized quickly that the cowboys were hams and relished the idea of playing around in front of an audience. But Ross, the one who had lived this life for twenty years, was standing as rigid as a flagpole.

"Hey, loosen up," she said, moving beside him.

"Easy for you to say. You're good at this."

She couldn't help but laugh. With all of his experience, the man acted as if he'd never been on stage before. "Let's go," she said. "The easiest way to deal with this is to start."

She turned to the crowd of cowboys. "Okay, boys," she called. "Everyone take a seat and let's read our parts together. If you're sharing a role with someone, sit together, and let's get a feel for how everything is going to flow."

Sugar smiled up at Ross. "You sit by me."

"You'd better believe it. I'm expecting you to pull me out of this hole I've dug for myself," he said, his lips twitching wryly.

Trace, the cowboy who had been the first to leave the earlier audition, had been the first to show up once the new plan was formulated. He was going to play one of the cowboys who tried to win Sugar's heart away from Ross, and as he took a seat, he grinned at them. "Heck, Ross, there ain't nothing to be nervous about. If you want me to I can show you how to kiss Sugar for the finale."

Deep down, Sugar had been wondering if that part of the role might be bothering Ross. She hadn't said anything about it, but she had wondered. Personally, she'd told herself this was a professional play and a romantic comedy, so a kiss in the end was expected. But there was no denying that just thinking about kissing Ross did funny things to her. Now, she glanced at him as he pinned Trace with a fierce look.

"I'm only teasing, bro," Trace added quickly, his own eyes laughing.

"Good." Ross took the seat beside Sugar on the edge of the stage. "After all, she wrote the role for me. Didn't you?"

The room seemed to shrink with his words, and Sugar nodded slowly. It was nothing more than the truth. Now she was the one who was nervous. "But, um, we aren't going to actually kiss, until the night of the play."

Ross arched his brow, and the lines around his eyes crinkled. "I don't know about that, I told you when I signed on for this that I'm not a very good actor. I'm going to want lots of chances to practice everything this script has in it."

The cowboys hooted with laughter, but looking into his eyes, Sugar wasn't sure if he was teasing her or not. And as she tore her gaze away and tried to focus on the rehearsal, she wasn't so sure she'd made a wise move when she'd written that kiss into the play. Kissing Ross Denton might just be the most dangerous thing she ever did.

What was he doing? Ross couldn't believe he had made that comment about kissing Sugar. And in front of the entire cast, too. He knew there wasn't a man in that barn who couldn't look at him and tell he was in over his head where Sugar was concerned. His one consolation after that was that his lines were written to be flubbed. He did one humdinger of a good job of it the rest of the night.

He wasn't certain if Sugar thought he was going along with the part, or if she realized he'd shaken himself up so badly he could hardly read the script.

Fortunately, aside from that predicament, the night went well. He actually had a good time. He was truly enjoying this production…as long as he didn't let himself remember every day that passed, he was digging himself into a deeper hole, falling for Sugar.

On Monday morning, Haley grinned across the office at Sugar as she said, "Will told me that practice got pretty interesting the other night."

Sugar grunted, having thought of little else all weekend. "He noticed, huh?"

"Everyone noticed, Sugar. You are the talk of the town. So, I have to ask—you sneak, did you write the kiss in so you could indeed kiss Ross?"

When Haley giggled, Sugar threw a paper wad at her. "This is not funny."

"Yes, it is. Did you seriously think when you named the character 'Hoss' that no one would think you were talking about Ross? I started to warn you about that. It was just too telling."

"Telling?"

"Yes, and you know it. That script wasn't just written as a play. It was a wish straight from your heart."

Sugar wanted to make a flip comment and push the very idea away with a joke, but she couldn't. "Haley," she said, "I'm leaving. Seriously. God opens that window for me just a crack, then I'm outta here, grabbing hold of my dream with both hands. I can't not."

Haley didn't look as if she believed her. And why should she? Sugar had heard the uncertainty in her own voice as she'd spoken the words that she'd said only a few weeks ago with such forceful assurance.

Sugar groaned in exasperation, slammed her elbows on her desk and dropped her head into her hands. "I am sooo not getting this!"

"Okay, now sweep me into your arms," Sugar instructed Ross. They'd been rehearsing the rest of the show all week long, and there just wasn't any way to avoid the last scene any longer. Every day that she put it off just made it all the more awkward.

From the edge of the stage, chuckles and silly coos broke out. Ross kept a straight face, but his eyes got all silky. Sugar's legs went weak as he stepped close. She swallowed hard when he ever so slowly slipped one arm around her waist and the other around her shoulders. Standing there, with his lips hovering next to her temple, she lost her train of thought.

"Like this?" he asked, his breath feathering across her skin. She nodded, frozen. "Don't you need to put your arms around me?" he added.

"Oh, yeah." She managed to lay one hand across his heart and the other around his waist. As soon as she did, he dipped one knee, bent her expertly, and instantaneously, she found herself in the perfect romantic dip. The room around them went dead silent. Sugar gasped, looking up at him and his eyes drifted over her face, lingered on her lips. He was going to kiss her! She closed her eyes…but nothing happened. One second she was cradled in his strong arms, and the next he'd popped her back onto her feet.

"So I guess that's how it's done," he said.

Her head was spinning. "Yes," she managed to mumble between clenched teeth. "I suppose that will have to do."

He looked at her with hooded eyes and smiled. "I guess you're right. Or we can try it again. You know how I like to practice."

That sent the entire cast hooting and hollering, reminding Sugar of their audience. She held up her hand like a flag, stopping him as he stepped toward her. "No! No need. I think this practice is over."

Applegate snorted loudly enough from up top that everyone turned his way. "Y'all need ta kiss and git this show on the road."

"Ain't that the truth," Stanley called from beside him. "And we ain't atalkin' about no stinkin' script."

Sugar laughed. What else was there to do? She looked at Ross and he chuckled, too. Thankfully, the tension eased.

Eased…but it did not disappear. When there was a ten-thousand-pound elephant in the room, there was just no way to make it vanish.

Chapter Seventeen

"Sugar Rae, where are you? Sugar!"

"Ross, what's wrong?" she asked. The show was in its second week of rehearsals, but she was alone in the dressing room. There was no rehearsal that night because of a cattle auction in the next county. Now, at the urgent tone in Ross's voice, Sugar jumped up and hurried out onto the stage. "I thought you'd still be at the auction." She took in his drenched appearance as he stomped down the aisle toward her.

"The weather shut it down early. Do you not *hear* that?"

There was a really nice rain going on outside. "You mean the rain? I was listening to it while I sat in the dressing room, writing. You can hear it better on the tin roof there, because it's lower than out here. You won't believe it, but I'm writing another play! It just hit me while I was painting the set..." She halted, realizing that Ross was staring at her as if she'd lost her mind. "Why are you looking at me like that?"

"This is not just rain. This is a storm. Small twisters are touching down all over the county. A tornado was just spotted about forty miles away, coming this direction."

"But it's been such a nice, calm rain," she said. Had she been so absorbed in her writing that she hadn't realized the change in the weather?

A brilliant flash of lightning lit the sky outside the barn windows and immediately thunder exploded, rattling the building.

She almost jumped off the stage.

"*That's* why I came looking for you," Ross shouted, over another blast of thunder.

Nope, it hadn't been like this ten minutes ago. No way would she have missed hearing this. She'd have crawled under the benches if she'd had any idea the storm was this bad.

"I had no idea," she called, hurrying to the edge of the stage. "Why are you out in this?"

Instead of answering, he grabbed her around the waist and lifted her from the stage. Setting her on the ground, he took her arm and led her toward the door. "I came looking for you. I couldn't get you to pick up your phone, and I was afraid you were either here or stranded somewhere on the side of the road."

He'd been *worried* about her. The thought momentarily made her forget what was going on around them... until the lights suddenly went out.

Ross pulled her close, wrapping a protective arm over her shoulders. "We'll take my truck," he shouted over the sound of the storm.

"But—"

"We'll get your car tomorrow. Right now, I'm driving you home." He pulled the door open and a gust of wind whipped rain in on them. Taking his hat off, he placed it on her head.

"Hang on to that for me," he called over another crack of thunder, tugging it low over her eyes. "I'm afraid I don't have anything else to help keep you dry. You ready? We're going to my side of the truck."

Sugar pressed her free hand on top of the hat, touched that he was trying to protect her. She gave a quick nod and then ran with him into the storm.

Even though he'd parked close to the barn entrance, they were still soaked by the time they reached his truck. He yanked open the door and had her inside before she had a chance to lift a foot. Gasping from the water and the wind, she scrambled over the console into the passenger's seat, jumping when a bolt of lightning and a simultaneous blast of thunder shook the vehicle.

Ross had come out into this madness looking for her, she realized as she watched him slide behind the wheel and slam his door. He'd been worried about her.

The idea wrapped around her like comforting arms. Seeing him drenched to the bone, water running from his hair and down his face because of *her,* she let the full implications of his actions sink in. This meant that…he cared.

She cared. She'd be lying if she denied it any longer. Knowing he'd come for her, seeing the worry in his eyes and recognizing the caring behind his actions undid her.

"You okay?" he shouted over the wind and yet another blast of thunder.

Still breathing hard, and not exactly sure if she would ever be okay again, she nodded and blotted water from her eyes. "Where did this come from? I had no idea it had gotten so bad." The roof and walls of the truck muffled the sound of the storm enough to allow for conversation.

He wiped his face with his hand as he backed away from the barn. "They can blow in pretty quickly here. Like I said, there have been sightings of twisters touching down in the county. And we're under a tornado watch."

Sugar shivered and studied the violent sky. Water was rushing across the roads, but Ross's four-wheel drive sliced though it smoothly. That wouldn't have been so easy in her old car. The town looked eerily empty when they turned onto Main Street. It, too, had lost power, and not a single light shone anywhere.

He drove slowly down the dark and deserted street. "I'm not leaving you alone in that apartment," he said over the swish of wipers working at full speed. There was a reprieve from lightning and thunder at the moment, but the rain was relentless.

"I'll be okay," she said, not feeling exactly confident about walking up those stairs to her dark apartment.

"I'm not leaving, not while a tornado watch is in effect. How about I take you to Adela's apartment house. We can wait the storm out there."

He'd started heading toward the Victorian at the end of town when headlights cut through the night. "That's Brady."

Both men pulled to a halt and rolled down their

windows. Water rushed in with punishing force. "What's up?" Ross shouted over the roar of the storm.

"Portion of the roof blew off the women's shelter," his friend yelled. "I came to the office to get more emergency tarps. I could use your help."

"Lead the way," Ross yelled back without hesitating. He closed the window and turned to face Sugar. "You want me to drop you off—"

She shook her head. "No! I'll go, too. Maybe I can help."

He nodded, then concentrated on turning the truck in the buffeting wind. They followed Brady through the night, his taillights barely visible through the torrent. Sugar sat in silence and worried about all the ladies from the candy store who lived at the shelter with their children. Surely no one had been harmed when part of the roof was ripped away, or Brady would have said something.

The lights of the house were out as they drove down the lane, but several other trucks were also pulling into the yard as they approached. Their headlights glowed faintly through the storm. Brady must have put out a call for help.

A dozen or so cowboys in yellow slickers climbed out of their trucks. Some were pulling ladders from the beds.

"Are you going up on the roof in all this lightning?" Sugar asked Ross. It was a silly question, because it was apparent that was exactly what was about to happen. But she couldn't help being nervous about it.

He nodded, glancing toward the roof. "Don't look so worried. We'll be okay. We've worked in worse than this."

"You have?" she shouted over the thunder.

"Well, sure. When your cows, your land or your neighbors are in trouble, you have to go out no matter what the conditions."

"But where is your raincoat?" Not that it would do him any good in this, but she couldn't stop herself from worrying about him.

"I had something a little more important on my mind than a raincoat when I came into this earlier."

Sugar let his meaning sink in. He'd had getting to *her* on his mind, not grabbing the raincoat she'd seen hanging beside his back door. Her heart fluttered weakly.

"You ready?" he asked, and at her nod, he added, "Wait, and I'll come around and get you."

She loved his gallantry, but he had more important things to worry about at the moment than walking her to the door. "You go do your thing, Sir Galahad. I'll be fine. I'll head straight to the house." Before he could protest, she opened the door and jumped out.

The ground felt like a kiddy pool filled with mud. Rivers of water coursed across the driveway as she stared down at her submerged feet. The good news was that she had on plain rubber flip-flops; the bad news was she couldn't see them for the mud. She was glad she'd set Ross's hat on the seat or it would have been ripped from her head by the wind. She slogged through the mud and water, but only made it to the front of the truck before her determined hero swept her into his arms.

"Hold on," he growled, storming across the yard.

Oh, she could do that, all right. She'd been in this

embrace before, and hadn't been able to forget about it. Sugar wrapped her arms around his neck and did just as he asked.

He set her on the porch. "There you go." His voice was gentle and reassuring over the storm. "Inside now, and don't come back out. Be safe."

He was telling her to be safe? He was about to climb onto a two-story building! In the middle of a raging storm! She grabbed his arm before he could turn away, and pulled him back, hugging him tight. "*You* be safe," she whispered into his ear, then stepped away. She said a prayer for him and the other men as she turned to enter the house.

Dottie was holding the door open for her. "Get in here, girl. I can't believe you're out in this!"

"I didn't even know it was coming," Sugar said, walking in and accepting a towel from one of the other women. "Ross had to come rescue me from the barn." She wiped her face and scrubbed some of the water out of her hair as she explained how they'd encountered Brady.

"Well, I know this isn't the best of circumstances, but we're glad you're here. But, we have to get you into some dry clothes—which we happen to have plenty of in the back room."

Sugar slipped out of her flip-flops, wiped her feet with the towel and followed Dottie down the hall by the light of an oil lamp. Within minutes, she had on clean, dry clothes and was back in the kitchen with a hot cup of coffee in her hands. "You folks are prepared," she said.

They had oil lanterns, flashlights and an emergency generator.

"Around here, we believe in being ready for anything," Dottie said.

Sugar felt guilty as she stood there in the kitchen of No Place Like Home, enjoying their hospitality. Sure, she'd spoken with the ladies, even gone and bought some candy at the store where they all worked, but had she given any thought to what a wonderful place this was? Had she ever stopped to consider that there might be something she could do to help? Why, the room where she'd just exchanged her wet clothes for dry ones had been well stocked with items for women and children. What a ministry.

Maybe she could find a way to get involved with helping the shelter while she was here.

It was pretty impressive how Dottie used talents as a candy maker and a businesswoman to teach the residents both a marketable skill and a lot of knowledge they would need to open their own small business if they wanted.

Sugar felt a growing desire to help out as she visited with them and sipped her simple cream-and-sugar coffee.

In Beverly Hills she'd been so busy, so caught up in the fast pace she lived, scrambling from work to auditions and acting classes, that she'd never taken the time to think about giving back. But here in Mule Hollow, she felt a sense of community that she'd never experienced before. She realized how disconnected she'd always been. Ross had tried to get that point across to her, and it suddenly came through loud and clear.

She'd barely settled into a corner of a small couch when one of the small toddlers climbed into her lap. He was a darling, with dark hair and big blue eyes.

Dottie sat down beside her. "They just heard announced on the radio that the tornado warning is over. Thank the Lord. Maybe the wind will calm down and I can stop worrying about someone being blown off the roof."

"I'm with you." Sugar sighed, looking up from the little boy snuggled in her arms toward the dark windows streaming with rain. She prayed again for everyone's safety and wondered what Ross was doing. She wished she could be out there helping him.

"You seem so calm," Sugar said.

"I've been through much worse," Dottie explained. "I lived on the Florida coast. My home collapsed on me during a hurricane."

Sugar was amazed by the revelation. "I'd be a wreck right now if something like that had happened to me."

Dottie smiled. Her face reminded Sugar of a delicate china doll: porcelain skin, deep navy eyes and midnight-black hair. But aside from her beauty, there was a peace about Dottie that seemed to reach out to everyone around her. "I learned while I was buried in all that debris that God is in control of my life, even at the very worst of times. I still marvel at how He saved me and then orchestrated my life to bring me here. The Bible says it, and He proved it to me when He brought me to Mule Hollow. The minute I saw Brady, we connected. If not for a hurricane, I would have missed finding him and my baby." She laid her hand on her rounded stomach and smiled. "Do you want children, Sugar?"

It was an unexpected question. "Someday," she answered with all honesty. Husband, family...it would all come—later. "I've always thought in terms of my career first. My plan is to make my dreams come true, become a star, and then think about a husband and children."

Dottie was studying her intently, as if looking deep into her soul. It was very disconcerting.

"Your career is everything to you, isn't it?"

Sugar didn't like the way that sounded. "No, it's not *everything*. It's what God's prepared me for. He put this dream inside me, and I'm determined to see it through. I feel in my heart that I'm meant to be a star." She knew she sounded like a broken record as she gave the same defensive explanation she'd given all her life. Suddenly, repeating it to Dottie, in this roomful of women living in this place of sanctuary Dottie had created, it sounded almost embarrassing. Still, it didn't change Sugar's conviction.

Dottie's expression wasn't judgmental, but her eyes were serious. "Do you mind if I ask you something?"

Sugar felt a sense of dread settle over her. Dottie had the kindest expression on her face, but Sugar had a sinking feeling she wouldn't like this question. Still, she nodded, curious despite her apprehension.

"What would you do if God asked you to lay it down?"

Sugar felt as if she'd walked off the end of a pier. She had come to Mule Hollow to banish that horrible voice of doubt in her head, only to have Ross imply it, and now Dottie give voice to it.

"What do you mean?" She could hardly speak as the words swept from the shadows of her heart and roared to life with the fervor of the raging wind that buffeted the house. Was it just a coincidence that Dottie had asked such a question using those *exact* words?

"I'm not implying that what you've decided is wrong, I just want to ask you what would you do if God asked you to lay your dream down. Would you trust Him enough to do it?"

"Trust Him?"

"Yes. If He gave it to you…could you give it back to Him if He asked you to?"

"Why would He ask something like that? He put the dream inside me?"

Dottie's eyes softened. "When I ended up here, I didn't understand, either. I thought I knew my life plan. It was a noble one, but I had to give that over to God and trust that he knew what was best for me. I look at you, and I think about Abraham, who wanted a son so badly. When God blessed him with Isaac, he was asked that same question. And then, though Isaac was the fulfillment of his dream, God asked Abraham to give him up."

Outside, the storm seemed to be calming down and a sudden hush came over the room. Everyone had been involved in their own discussions, and yet Sugar felt exposed, just as she had the night Ross said that she was afraid. Yes, she'd confronted her fear of failure, her fear that somehow she'd been mistaken about what God wanted her to do. But to just say that her dream *was* what she was supposed to do, and then say that God was asking her to simply lay it down at the altar—could she do that?

Call her stubborn, but she couldn't accept that God would ask her to do that. She didn't want to hurt Dottie's feelings, or lessen her experience, but…

For a person fearing failure, accepting that God was telling her to lay her dreams down would actually be the easy way out. She wouldn't have to take personal responsibility for her failure. Could Sugar lay her dreams at the altar? In all truth, she wasn't sure. But she was sure of one thing: she wasn't copping out on her lifetime dream without a fight.

She wasn't taking the easy way out in any way, shape or form. It wasn't the way she operated. It never had been, and yet… Ross's image came to mind and Sugar's entire thought process froze up.

Chapter Eighteen

The tramp of boots on the porch signaled the men coming into the kitchen, and saved Sugar from answering Dottie's question aloud.

Stacy, who'd been sitting across the room, came forward when Sugar stood up. "I'll take him," she said quietly, reaching for the sleepy toddler.

"Thank you. He's really sweet."

The woman smiled briefly before she walked away. Sugar got the sense that Stacy had wanted to say something more, but when she didn't turn back, Sugar decided she must have just imagined it. Instead of dwelling on it, she hurried to the kitchen to see what she could do to help the tired, drenched men who stood dripping on the linoleum.

They were so wet the rain collected in puddles, but Dottie wouldn't let them go back onto the porch. "No," she said when they tried to retreat. "Don't even think about this old floor." She handed them each a towel and thanked them personally for their help.

Sugar passed out cups of coffee, then moved to stand beside Ross when everyone had been served. She'd been worrying about him the entire time she was talking with Dottie, and she'd almost thrown her arms around him when he came through the doorway, safe and sound. But she didn't need any more little hints and speculations about them falling for each other, so instead she contented herself with standing close by his side, listening to him talk with the other men.

Despite the roof damage and the harrowing conditions they'd just faced, the men were in good spirits as they talked and sipped their hot drinks.

One of them was dress-store owner Ashby Templeton's fiancé, Dan Dawson. The striking cowboy oozed mischievous "Matthew McConaughey" charm.

"Friend, I thought you were dead meat out there when you slipped," he said, looking at Ross.

Alarm slammed into Sugar. "What happened?"

Ross paused in running a towel over his hair, and shot her a rueful smile. "It wasn't that bad. My foot slipped when I was tacking the edge of the tarp."

Her heart stopped, knowing how steep and high that roof was.

"At the *top* of the roofline," Dan stated. "Only the Lord saved him from plummeting off the edge."

Ross shot him a warning glare.

"Hey, I'm just saying I'm glad you're still with us." Dan grinned, winking at Sugar before joining a conversation with the guys on his left.

Sugar looked at Ross.

"It was nothing," he said in a low voice, turning toward her. "Would it have mattered to you?"

She got a mental picture of him tumbling off that slick roof, and her stomach rolled right along with him. It shook her to realize just how much it would have mattered. She looked up at him and nodded. "Yes," she said. "Very much," she added.

Ross's surprise was palpable. He clearly hadn't expected her to admit that. Sugar was just as astounded at the admission. She blamed it on her conversation with Dottie.

"Well," he said, swallowing hard. "I'm fine. The roof is protected and the storm is almost over. God's good."

Sugar took a deep breath and nodded.

God was good. But she was beginning to wonder if she understood Him at all. She was suddenly wondering if she understood *anything*.

Ross pulled up in front of Sugar's apartment. The rain had stopped, but mist still hung in the air, seeming as undecided and frustrated about its next move as Ross. He glanced at the dashboard clock. One-thirty in the morning. It had been a long, eye-opening night.

Coming face-to-face with his mortality up on that building had shaken him. He hadn't wanted to let anyone else know exactly how close a call he'd had up on that slick roof, but when his foot slipped and he went sliding down those shingles, it *had* been an act of God that he'd not ended up going over the edge. That his boot had caught the lip of the gutter and the gutter had held…well, he was giving the good Lord all the glory on that one.

Sugar's admission that what happened to him mattered to her had caused his adrenaline to pump even more furiously than it had as he plunged toward certain disaster on that roof. When she'd said that standing there beside him, he'd wanted to draw her close and hug her. He'd held back, though. He was soaked to the bone and she'd changed into dry clothes, not to mention he was sure she wouldn't have welcomed the advance.

He'd been fooling himself for weeks now. In spite of all his attempts to guard his heart, he cared about Sugar. He was obviously a glutton for heartache, because that was the only place this could take him.

"Are you going to be okay?" he asked, fighting off the urge to reach out and touch her now. She'd been quiet the entire drive into town. She nodded and started to open her door. He hopped out of the truck and reached her just as she closed her door behind her.

She stepped up onto the sidewalk. He followed, not wanting the night to end. At the bottom of the stairs she paused, her hand on the railing as she turned toward him. "You came to find me tonight."

"Yeah, I did." All he'd been able to think about when he couldn't get her on the phone was that she might not be safe. Just as she, apparently, had worried about him while he was out on the roof.

She'd admitted that it would have mattered to her if he'd fallen, but he knew her confession was bothering her. Still, that fact gave him a little glimmer of hope.

He'd read her like an open book after she'd made the

admission. She didn't want to care for him any more than he wanted to care for her.

They were standing in the beam of his headlights, and her eyes seemed huge as she looked up at him. His throat went dry.

"Why did you come after me?" she asked, her words barely a whisper.

Why? That's what a man who loves a woman does— Ross had been in denial about it almost as long as he'd known her, but as he slid down that slick roof he'd known he couldn't deny it anymore. At least, not to himself. "I'm your hero, remember?"

She smiled. "Cute. But really?"

There was *no way* he could tell her he loved her. He was still trying to get his mind around it himself! Besides, he knew she would be unhappy if he told her. "Why wouldn't I come after you?"

Her eyes kind of melted in the truck light, as if maybe she liked the way that sounded. But, no, she was probably just tired. "Y-you and me," he said, fumbling for the right cover-up. "W-we're friends. You don't want me falling off roofs, and I don't want roofs falling on your head." *Well, that was lame.*

"Oh. Right," she said, nodding. "Thanks for that. G-good night, then."

He snapped his arms across his chest, locking his hands between his biceps and his ribs. It was the only way to keep from reaching for her.

"I've been thinking," she said, swinging around suddenly, her eyes flashing. "I've enjoyed working with you." She looked and sounded as if she were fighting to keep her balance on a tightrope. Or maybe it just seemed that way to him, since that was how he was feeling.

"I've enjoyed working with you, too," he stated. "I need to admit something—I didn't have any desire to do this production. As you know, I didn't want anything to do with it. But I've enjoyed myself more than I could ever have imagined."

She smiled. "I thought so. I mean, well, I thought you were enjoying the production part of it. You know, getting things started. I know you haven't enjoyed the acting part."

He relaxed. "I've even enjoyed that."

"Oh."

That made him grin. "You're speechless. Wow."

She chuckled.

"We have created something special, Sugar. Because you pushed me to do this, I feel closer to Grandpop than I ever have. I know where he got his love and drive from now. It came from the pride of taking something from the ground up and building it into a legacy."

"So, does that mean you're going to keep the theater open for certain?"

He'd led her to believe he wasn't in it for the long haul—made as little commitment as possible, but that had all changed. "I am," he said. "I know you're not going to stay here, but I was hoping you might want to remain a partner in it." He hadn't realized he was going to say this, but now that it was out, he knew it was right. The financials he and Sugar had worked out had only been for the immediate future, but he wanted some way to stay connected to her, some way that would keep the door open for her to come back.

She looked thoughtful. "Out there tonight at the shelter, I realized you were right. You know, about me not having a life of any kind outside of achieving my dream."

"I was rough on you. I didn't tell you that your passion for what you do impresses me. Your dedication, your commitment to it...inspires me. Yes, I said your *commitment* to it. I know that will steal you away from our theater here, but I understand it."

She blinked rapidly, her eyes glistened in the headlights. "Coming from you that means a lot to me."

He wished it meant enough to keep her here. Wished he could tell her how he really felt. But he couldn't. "You're one of the most talented people I've ever known. In God's timing, you're going to make it. I know I've been hard on you, but that's the way I see it."

She took a deep breath and then threw her arms around him and hugged him fiercely. "I needed to hear that. Thank you." She let go abruptly, then jogged up the stairs. He watched her as she switched on the emergency light he'd given her and then unlocked her door. She gave him a small smile before disappearing inside.

He stood there, still looking at her screen door as he gathered his wits about him.

He'd worked and acted with Sugar for the last few weeks, and he'd never been around anyone he thought had more reason to believe in her God-given talent than she did. There was no doubt in his mind that Sugar was destined to be a star.

It was only a matter of time. All she needed was the right moment, the right opportunity, and she was going to soar....

Right out of his life.

The damage to the county wasn't nearly as bad as it could have been. Several people had trees down and some damage to shingles, but no one had anything worse than the shelter's ripped-up roof. Overall, Mule Hollow residents felt relieved and blessed that all they'd received from the storm was a few small twisters and not an actual tornado.

Sugar joined in the next day as many of the townspeople pitched in to clean the shelter's yard of debris. The insurance adjuster came out and gave his estimate, and no sooner had he left than Ross, jokester Dan Dawson and several other men, including a quiet cowboy named Emmett, joined Brady on the roof to start replacing shingles.

There was plenty of work still to be done on the show. Sugar could have easily left and gone out to the barn. There were so many people working at the shelter that she wouldn't have been missed, but she realized she wanted to help. She wanted to participate. This was a community that cared about each other. These were her friends, they needed her help and she gladly gave it.

At the moment, lending a helping hand was more important than her production.

She went to the side of the house to pick up shingles from the playground area, and saw Stacy was working there also. Sugar noticed the woman's gaze flicker up, keeping track of Emmett on that steep roofline. Sugar found herself doing the same thing with Ross. She was terrified he might lose his footing again, though she realized it was a senseless fear. The man was very capable.

His words from the night before had sent her into a tailspin. He believed in her! That admission alone had almost made her burst into tears. But knowing that she'd been right about his loving the work on the production pleased her even more. And the show would go on even after she left Mule Hollow. That meant more to her than she'd thought possible. She was so proud of what they were creating.

"I think it's wonderful how you can get up on that stage in front of all those people."

Sugar had been so absorbed in her thoughts that she hadn't heard Stacy move closer to her. Startled that the shy woman had actually spoken an entire sentence, Sugar went blank for a minute. "I love it," she said, a heartbeat later.

"It would terrify me."

"Have you ever tried it?" *Of course she hadn't tried it. The woman didn't talk!*

"No. I never could. I wouldn't be good at it, anyway."

Sugar tossed a broken shingle into the nearby wheelbarrow and, then, instead of reaching for another one, gave Stacy her full attention. "You know, sometimes getting out there on that stage, or in front of a camera, is a freeing experience. You might be surprised by what you could do while playing a role, that you couldn't do as yourself."

It was true. Sugar knew firsthand; she'd been living for the hours she and Ross could be on stage and she could let herself be the woman who was falling in love with him. Suddenly, she was inspired with an idea. "Would you like to come out to the theater one night and help me go over lines? Maybe try it out?"

Stacy went white. "Oh, no. I couldn't. I—"

"You'd be surprised at how many actors and actresses are really shy people." Sugar had this sudden determination to get Stacy to at least come out to the barn.

"Really?" She didn't look as if she believed it, but seemed to be thinking it over. "How can that be?"

"Well, it's certainly not true of me—I've been a camera hog all my life—but for some it's a way of expressing themselves."

Stacy gave Sugar a small smile. "I'm a long way from a camera hog. But I might come out and maybe let you read your lines to me, if you need someone to do that."

Sugar got the most unbelievable sensation in the pit of her stomach, as if something very significant had just happened, something larger than herself. Oddly, she found it hard to speak. She nodded instead, swallowed and then met Stacy's gaze with a smile. A smile she felt from her heart. She found her voice then. "Tomorrow. Right after work. No one else gets there until seven. I really could use your help."

"Maybe I'll come, if no one else is going to be there."

Sugar decided right then and there that she would

make sure no one else was around. Applegate and Stanley showed up early every once in a while to fiddle with things, but she knew that for Stacy, they'd stay away. "It'll just be you and me. And I know we're going to have fun. You'll see."

They worked a few minutes more, finishing the clean-up around the playground before Stacy went inside to check on her toddler. Sugar looked up at the men hammering away on the roof, and waved when she saw Ross watching her. Her heart was full to bursting suddenly, and at the same time she felt immensely lighthearted.

Chapter Nineteen

"Okay, I'm Hoss, and you're me. Sweet little ole Daisy Calhoun," Sugar said, smiling. She and Stacy had been at the barn for an hour, and Sugar could tell the reserved woman was enjoying herself even if it wasn't especially visible. But Sugar had this burning desire to pull the energy she sensed inside of Stacy out into the open.

She'd asked Haley about Stacy, and found out she'd had an extremely sad life. Abuse was something Sugar had never known, and after her conversation with Haley, she'd taken off from work thirty minutes early to come to the barn where she could be alone. She had had the intense impression that she should pray before Stacy arrived. She had asked God to please be in the barn with them.

Looking into the deer-in-the-headlights eyes that Stacy had just leveled on her, Sugar prayed she wasn't doing the wrong thing by pushing her out onto the stage. But it felt right. She wanted Stacy to know how the stage made her feel.

"Don't look so scared," she said, then added encouragement. "You can do this. Remember, it's just you and me. And most of all, this is *fun*. When you step onto this stage..." Sugar walked out into the middle of the space and took a deep breath, her eyes closed. "It is all about what's happening here. Nothing out there matters." She opened her eyes and looked at Stacy. "Right here, you don't have to think about who you are. What your problems are. What your shortcomings are—not that we have any," she added with a teasing grin. "Right here, it's all about the character. It's about breathing life into your role so that the audience is transported away from *their* troubles."

Stacy's hands trembled as she gripped the script. She didn't say anything, but her gaze fell to the pages in her hands. Sugar was holding her breath and praying God would somehow use her to help this wounded soul out of her shell.

"Okay, I'll try."

Sugar wanted to grab Stacy up in a big hug, but was afraid she'd scare the poor girl, so she held back and smiled instead. "That's all any of us can do. Now, from the top, Daisy girl. 'Hoss is so in love with you he needs you to put him out of his misery and tell him that ya luv him!'"

"Oh, Ross, it was unbelievable. I have never, and I mean never, felt as excited and fulfilled as when Stacy read my lines like she was Daisy!"

Ross was speechless, looking at the exhilaration radiating from Sugar. It didn't help his situation at all. He'd been in complete knots since the night of the storm; knowing that he loved her enough to want her to fulfill her dream even if it meant watching her fly away from him was stretching him thin. But looking at her now, something was different. He could feel it. He smiled as she grabbed him and hugged him, before swinging away like a twirling top.

She'd cornered him the moment he'd arrived, and pulled him to the side of the barn, away from the other cast members.

"I always had this dream that I was supposed to be up on the big screen so that I could make a difference in some kid's life. You know, like what happened with me. But I never thought about using my love of acting in a one-on-one situation. I really think I can help Stacy come out of her shell."

"Sugar, if there is one thing I know for sure, it's that you can bring out the actor in anyone."

She was standing three feet away from him, her eyes alive with hope. He knew he'd never seen anything more beautiful in all of his life.

"It'll take time. Stacy won't be up there acting anytime soon—who knows, she may never want to act in front of people. Even if she doesn't, it is still a great thing. She walked out of here today with what I truly think was a lilt in her step."

"You did good, Sugar."

She looped her arm through his and turned her smiling face up to him. "Not me. God did it. I could *feel* Him. He was right there beside me."

Ross couldn't help it, he placed his free hand on the side of her face, cherishing the texture of her skin. He'd fallen in love with this woman's passion and her spirit. "God's going to use you in a great way, Sugar. With your talent and your beautiful heart, there is no telling what He has in store for you. I see greatness in you."

She went totally still, her eyes growing troubled. "Yeah, that's what I've always felt," she said, but there was no note of bragging in her tone. "You know me, I'm sure as shootin' supposed to be America's next sweetheart."

For the first time since he'd known her, she didn't say the words with conviction. He didn't know how to feel about that.

"Yup, ya got that right," he teased, trying to lift the suddenly solemn mood hanging over them. He started walking her toward the front of the barn, needing to join the crowd before he broke down and kissed her. "It's time for practice. You know how I need it."

She chuckled at that and squeezed his arm. "You're so much better than you think."

"Only because I have you up there beside me."

And that was the truth. He was supposed to be Hoss the singing cowboy when he was acting out his part, but that was him, Ross Denton, up on that stage—the man who loved Sugar Rae Lenox, heart and soul. Once she headed off to her destiny, he was going to go back behind the scenes and let the others do the performing. Without her, he didn't want to be on stage.

Who was he kidding? Without her, he didn't want to be anywhere.

* * *

There was a church social on Sunday morning after service. In the words of Applegate, Mule Hollow knew how to "put on the dog." Sugar hoped dog wasn't on the menu, but there was so much barbecued meat on the table, one could never know for sure.

After she filled her plate, Sugar sat at a table with several couples. Before long, Ross came and settled beside her. Everyone at the table was joking and talking and having a good time. Her shoulder was pressed to Ross's for most of the meal, and she was so very aware of him. So much that she was relieved when he went to change for volleyball.

Mule Hollow volleyball was unique and unlike anything Sugar had ever seen—or rather, the dress code was. It was pure entertainment to see both the men and women.

While some of the cowboys changed into shorts and athletic shoes, others opted to play in their dress attire: Western shirts, stiff starched jeans and cowboy boots! And then there were Esther Mae and her husband, Hank—him sporting full-dress attire and her in a lime-green jersey. The group was rounded off with Norma Sue's husband, Roy Don. He served as the referee, and fittingly so, as he was a stout cowboy with a full mustache and commanding presence. He was starched up stiff as concrete from the bottom of his tan jeans to the collar of his pearl-snap dress shirt.

Looking at them, Sugar had no doubt that Mule Hollow most assuredly made a fashion statement. But it was Norma Sue, running roughshod over everyone as she organized the game like a general, who took the prize for best dressed. She wore her trademark overalls with the legs rolled up to just below her knees, and instead of sneakers, she, too, kept on her boots. She topped the look off with a red sweatband that came just above her eyebrows and made her short gray hair bush out all over the place.

Sugar was standing to one side, watching in wonder, when Ross jogged over to her. He had opted for athletic wear.

"Hey," he said, stepping close. "Are you going to hang around?"

She nodded, smiling at him. Wild horses couldn't drag her away from watching him—and the others. "Is Norma Sue going to play like that?"

He chuckled. "She always does. And surprising as it may be, that short dynamo can hold her own out there. The woman has a mean serve." His eyes were twinkling with merriment.

Sugar felt happy just from looking at him. "How about you? Can you play?"

"I do all right. How about you?"

She shook her head. "Not my game. But I'll really enjoy cheering you on."

He leaned close. "With you cheering me on, they had better watch out. I'll be unstoppable." He was just so appealing that Sugar did what came naturally before she thought better of it. She rose up on her toes and kissed him.

It was just a simple touch of the lips, but it felt like so

much more that both of them froze. They'd been dancing around kissing each other for weeks.

Ross didn't move, but his eyes were not twinkling as they held hers. "That was a dangerous move right there, Sugar."

Boy, did she know it. But suddenly she was tired of dancing. "And what does that mean?" She could hardly breathe.

"It means I've been playing this game between us with a handicap, trying to give you room to make up the rules. Fair warning—don't kiss me unless you're willing to change them."

And that was the million-dollar question. Did she want the rules to change?

Yes.

"Ross Denton, you gonna play or what? Get out here," Norma Sue hollered. "We've got a game to play and daylight's aburnin'."

He lifted a questioning brow and Sugar took a shuddering breath. "Go play ball." She pushed him lightly and he backed away toward the players.

"This conversation isn't over." He gave her a smile of warning. "You and me, after this game." He pointed at himself, then her, as he said it.

She couldn't help but chuckle. "Play. Ball. Tough guy."

He grinned full out. "Oh, yeah, I'm goin' to go out there and keep the games movin' faster than you can blink. And then you and me are havin' a heart-to-heart." He winked, then spun and jogged away.

As she watched him join the others, Sugar sank to the

grass. Her legs wouldn't hold her up. *What, oh what was she doing?*

She'd been having trouble all week. Ever since the storm, really, but it was the night when she'd talked with him after helping Stacy that something inside of her had switched gears. She'd been flirting with danger and she knew it. She'd been attracted to him from day one, of course, but he'd said the most beautiful things to her that night. He really believed in her. And he really wanted her to reach her dream. He hadn't said so, but she could tell he had deep feelings for her.

And then there was the kissing issue. They'd practiced their final scene all this time and never actually kissed. She had known he was barely holding back, and it had driven her crazy.

And now she'd crossed a line.

"Sooo, what's the story?" Lacy asked, plopping down on the grass beside her. "You are looking at that cowboy like he's a glass of water and you've been lost in the desert for a week."

Sugar jerked her eyes away from watching Ross stretch for a high ball. He looked great. "What story? There isn't any story."

Lacy smiled, stretched her legs out on the grass and crossed her feet. "Mmm-hmm if that's your version, I'm cool. I just wanted to come say thanks for giving some of your time to Stacy. I make it a point to try and draw her out, but it has been a slow process. I really got excited when she told me she had fun reading with you on Monday night, and that y'all are going to do it again. Just so you know, she really enjoyed it. You could be an answer to a prayer with what you're doing. What you did, giving her your time, was a big blessing, Sugar."

Sugar's heart lifted at the knowledge. "You know, Lacy, it was a blessing for me, more than Stacy will ever know. I have never felt that way before, sharing something that means so much to me with someone else. And I think with time, and given half a chance, she might get up on that stage and perform herself."

Lacy's blue eyes widened and her smile flashed, like a child in awe of a Christmas tree. "That would be a miracle in so many ways. You're good for Mule Hollow, Sugar. I hope you know that. I mean, I know you have plans to go back to L.A. After seeing your ability, I understand totally that you could be famous tomorrow." She paused and picked a blade of Bermuda grass before pegging Sugar with intense eyes. "Or maybe God has prepared you for a different kind of fame than you thought."

Six weeks ago—even two weeks ago—Sugar would have been frustrated by such a remark. But she knew Lacy had a missionary's heart. Lacy had come to Mule Hollow to open her salon so that she could be a witness to the women who moved to the town. Lacy had a heart for souls.

Sugar sighed. The answer she always gave didn't come. Her throat clogged, instead. She'd been so excited about getting the show up and running so that she could garner her reviews and then move on to bigger and better things…but was there anything bigger and better than what she'd felt here, in this tiny town?

"You sure make Ross happy," Lacy said, breaking into her thoughts.

Sugar looked toward the volleyball court, automatically seeking him out. *He made her happy.* He was in the back row at the moment, and despite the rambunctious volleying in progress with the black-and-white ball, she found him watching her instead of the game. Their eyes locked and her stomach did a roll-over-and-die maneuver. He was looking at her as if he loved her, and she knew that as long as she lived, nothing within the bounds of human possibilities could compare with that. Someone shouted his name and Ross jerked his attention back to the game just as the volleyball shot across the net and hit him between the eyes—or would have if a lime-green flash of waving arms and legs squealing, "mine-mine-mine" hadn't flown into him first.

Chapter Twenty

From his prone position in the sand, Ross popped one eye open and looked up at the crowd circling him. His ankle was killing him, his right eye was swelling and throbbing, he couldn't breathe and there was a crushing pain on his chest—a bright green one!

Thankfully someone reached out and helped Esther Mae off of him so he could finally get some air. But then Sugar's face came into focus—in his good eye—and he lost his breath again.

"Oh, Ross, you look terrible. What can I do?" she asked, sinking onto the sand beside him.

He thought he could see everyone behind her grinning, but then again, he wasn't focused on anything but her. Ready to blame it on getting knocked senseless by Esther Mae's right hook, he grinned at Sugar and said the first thing that popped into his addled brain. "You can marry me."

Yup, he'd lost his ever lovin' mind. And he didn't care one iota.

She blinked, and the crowd went silent.

"Ain't ya gonna say sump-thin', Sugar?" Applegate bellowed after a couple of seconds. "Ross, 'bout time ya finally come to yor senses. Pity it took a beatin' from Esther Mae ta do it!"

Sugar still didn't say anything.

Applegate didn't give up. "I was beginin' ta thank them two didn't have a lick a sense b'twin the both of 'em," he said to the group. "Thangs are lookin' up."

"Sugar?" Ross said, sitting up slowly. His ankle was still killing him, but the look in her eyes was ten times worse. He'd been a first-class fool. He'd gone and rushed her. He could see her shutting down. "Say something."

"I don't know what to say."

"Aw," Stanley groaned. "Now that jest ain't right."

"Come on, everyone," Lacy called, "let's give these two some breathing room. How about we open up the ice cream?"

Ross could have hugged the woman as everyone followed her lead and retreated toward the shade trees, where freezers of homemade ice cream sat hardening up in rock salt and ice.

"I'm not kidding, Sugar," Ross said, once they were alone. She stood up and stepped away from him. He tried to follow her, but his ankle gave way and he hobbled.

"That ankle needs ice," she said, then lifted his arm and drew it across her shoulders. "Lean on me, and let's take care of that."

He didn't care about his ankle, but he wasn't going to complain about the excuse to hold her. Then again, he knew he wasn't going anywhere on his own, what with the way his ankle was swelling. Esther Mae had really done a number on him.

No more, though, than Sugar had the moment she'd come to town.

There was a chair beside the blue ice chest, and he eased into it while Sugar pulled another chair over and carefully lifted his foot onto it. She wasn't looking at him. "Take your shoe off while I wrap some ice for you."

"Yes, dear," he said, smiling even though he was terrified. He knew this was right. Sugar was supposed to be with him. He got his shoe off and watched her yank a towel from a nearby table. Her movements were jerky.

"I can't believe you asked me to marry you," she said, filling the dish towel with ice.

"That's what someone in love does, Sugar."

She finally met his eyes as she gently laid the ice on his ankle. Her hands were trembling.

"If you love me, Sugar, then we can make this work. I don't care if you go off to Hollywood and make movies—well, actually, I do care about the kissing. I don't want you kissing anyone but me—but as long as I know you're coming home to me, then I can handle it. I want more than life itself to do this."

"Ross," she said, standing and pacing. "It just isn't that easy. Sure, everything has somehow changed since I got here but—"

"Do you love me?" He wished he could get up.

She slapped a hand to her hip. "Yes. And you good and well know it, cowboy. But you are not playing fair."

He was grinning, his heart was bursting and, sprained ankle and all, he was out of his chair. "I'm not, I admit it. I tried—but who's talking fair? You're the one who stole my heart, the one who wouldn't quit until you had me working beside you. I couldn't help but fall for you after that. You're the one who kept at me until I started to dream." He took her hand. "We're building something *here*, you and me. Yes, I believe God is going to use you in a great way, I do. But I was doing some thinking out there during the game, while I was looking at you—right before Esther Mae whacked some sense into me. Maybe God put me in your life to be your support. To stand by you and help you. And have you do the same for me."

He was talking a blue streak, trying to get it all out, to say everything in his heart. Trying to find the right words that would get through to her. "I don't know, Sugar, there are so many things, so many positive things, going through my head that it would take me hours to get it all said. And I will, but you already know it all. In your heart, you know it." He took her face between his palms and looked into her eyes, willing her to see his every emotion he felt.

She nodded. "I do know. I've been living for my dream for so long. You were right, I've been living for the future for so long it's hard for me to just live for today."

"But God's given us today. Now. He hasn't promised us tomorrow. And I don't want to waste another minute without knowing you are mine."

"Oh, Ross, you make it sound so easy."

"I'm sure there will be times when it won't be. I'm

sure we'll have to compromise and look out for each other's best interests. But loving you…that's the easy part."

Sugar knew everything he said to her was true. In her heart, she'd known that her life had changed, taken a turn for the better. She just had to have the courage to accept all that God was offering her. She lifted her hands and slid them around Ross's neck. She saw his love in his eyes, and drew strength from it. This was right. She saw a future she'd never dreamed of. Possibilities she'd never thought of until he'd come into her life. She thought of what they were building at the theater, and how she could be a part of a community she loved. But mostly, she thought about how much she loved Ross. Dreams might come and go, but she was looking at the one she knew she wanted for keeps.

She smiled. "It might not always be easy," she warned.

He smiled back, sliding his hands around her shoulders and pulling her close. "I can handle it, remember? I'm your hero. Please put me out of my misery and say you'll marry me, so we can get this show on the road."

Sugar laughed and felt her world fall into place. "Oh, Ross, it's going to be a wonderful show, isn't it?"

"It's going to be a runaway hit," he whispered against her lips as he lowered her into a perfect dip and kissed her with all his heart.

And from across the lawn they got a standing ovation!

Epilogue

On opening night, Sugar Rae stood backstage with her heart in her throat. Everyone's efforts had paid off, and it was so unbelievable to see the full house. Tickets to the other shows for the weekend were almost sold out as well and while she had no illusions that this would always be the case, for opening weekend, it was a thrill to see. God was so good.

She peeked through the curtain, which Adela had made, and glanced up at the loft. Applegate and Stanley, looking like generals overseeing a battlefield, were checking out the crowd as they prepared to dim the lights. Ross had already called the cast and crew together for a prayer.

Sugar had added her own thank-you into the prayer, feeling so humbled, and overwhelmed at the same time, at how the town had jumped in to make this happen. The ladies from the shelter had set up a refreshment booth outside in a small air-conditioned trailer, and Norma Sue and Esther Mae were greeting everyone at the door and handing out programs. Lacy, Sheri and Haley were helping orchestrate behind-the-scenes details such as keeping Sugar calm and giving her a hand with costume changes, among a host of other small things that needed to be taken care of. Their husbands were overseeing the parking area.

And then there was Molly. She'd done an unbelievable job of hyping the show in her articles and was sitting out there now, smiling like a dark-haired answer to prayer, waving when she caught Sugar's eye. Her review the week before of the dress rehearsal had been almost too wonderful, but Ross had assured her the praise was every bit deserved.

Sugar looked up and saw Ross and Will shaking hands. Then Ross went over and clapped Applegate and Stanley on their shoulders, saying something encouraging to them before he headed her way. The show was about to begin.

Ross was smiling as he came down the stairs from the catwalk. "Are you ready?" he asked, his eyes warm with excitement.

He had been right about so many things. The endeavor was much more than she'd anticipated, but together, they'd worked everything out. She was so grateful for Ross. And so in love with him. She'd grown to love him more and more every day they'd worked together.

She took a deep breath. "I've been ready my entire life," she said, then walked into his arms and hugged him with her heart and soul.

"Hey, what's this?" he asked, wrapping his arms around her. Sugar laid her cheek against his heart and drew from the well of steadfast assurance she always found in his arms.

"You're trembling," he whispered against her ear.

She closed her eyes. "I'm okay. I just needed you to hold me for a minute. I need you to know how much this means to me. How much all you've done has meant to me. Thank you."

His arms tightened and she felt the brush of his lips against her hair. "I'm thankful God put you in my life, Sugar. I thank Him every day. I've had more fun getting this place going and sharing the experience with you than I've ever had before. Building this with you has been a dream come true."

They were both silent as the lights dimmed. "Are you ready?" he whispered against her ear. She saw Lacy and Haley smiling at her, waiting for her signal.

"Let's do this," Sugar said, looking up into Ross's loving eyes. Rising on her tiptoes, she kissed him before taking his hand in hers. Together they walked onto the stage to welcome everyone to the first performance of *The Cowboy Takes a Bride*.

They knew it was going to be the performance of a lifetime.

* * * * *

Dear Reader,

Thank you for joining me and the gang in Mule Hollow! As always, I hope this book entertained you and maybe even made you chuckle a time or two. I had fun telling Sugar and Ross's love story—since I do *love* watching people figure out God's plan in their lives! In THE COWBOY TAKES A BRIDE, both Ross and Sugar find out exactly how perfect God's plan is as their paths collide in my tiny Texas town.

I hope that if you are struggling with something in your life, like Ross and Sugar, you will trust God, and know that He will not leave you or forsake you. As God has been in my life and in the lives of my characters, so is God with you all the way, and in His perfect timing, you will be able to see clearly.

I love to hear from readers. You can reach me at PO Box 1125, Madisonville, Texas, 77864; through my Web site, debraclopton.com; or through the Steeple Hill offices. Check out my new blog for up-to-date things happening in my life and my books at debraclopton.blogspot.com.

God bless you, and until we see each other again, live, laugh and seek God with all your heart.

Debra Clopton

P.S. I hope you join me in early 2009 as the sparks continue in Mule Hollow. That's when Texas Ranger Zane Cantrell comes to town and brings someone's secret past with him!

QUESTIONS FOR DISCUSSION

1. The Mule Hollow series is written with a sense of community as its core. In THE COWBOY TAKES A BRIDE, Sugar Rae had never felt a sense of belonging or responsibility to a community before. How do you feel about your community? Do you get involved? How about with your local church?

2. Sugar was so determined and single-minded in her quest to achieve her dream that she was afraid to fail. How did she handle that fear once she confronted it?

3. Do you have a dream that you've struggled with? Do you believe God would give you a deep desire and then ask you to lay it down at His feet as your sacrifice?

4. Sugar got so caught up in reaching her dream that she sometimes forgot to live life in the now. Do you have balance in your life between living for today and preparing for tomorrow? What does the Bible say about this?

5. Sugar Rae had valid reasons for being convinced she was supposed to be an actress. How has your past influenced your dreams?

6. How about Sugar's family—do you believe they

acted badly in supporting her dream early on and then pulling back? Why do you think they did this?

7. Why did Ross not want to have anything to do with Sugar's production? Do you think he had valid reasons?

8. Sugar was convinced God had put her dream of being an actress in her heart, and when she couldn't reach it, she became frustrated at the Lord. In your own life have you ever felt this way? Some people believe you should never question the Lord. What are your thoughts?

9. The pastor pointed out to Ross that his life in the entertainment industry might have been only the preparation for this moment when he had the chance to step up and help Sugar attain her dreams. What do you think about this, both in the book and as it pertains to life as you've seen it?

10. Sugar wasn't one to totally immerse herself in the word, but on a day-to-day basis she had an ongoing dialogue with the Lord. He was always a variable in her life, whether she was upset, happy or struggling to understand. How would you define her relationship with God? Was it a healthy one? Do you find that when you struggle you are brought closer to the Lord?

11. At the volleyball game, Lacy told Sugar that she knew Sugar could be famous. But then she said, "Or maybe God has prepared you for a different kind of fame." What do you think Lacy meant? Do you believe God gave Sugar her dream so that it would lead her to Mule Hollow?

12. Sugar understood that Lacy had a missionary's heart, but she hadn't ever realized that *she* could use her talent in a similar manner until she encouraged Stacy to read the part in the play. Do you have abilities that you could use to show others God's love? How could you do this?

13. Sugar realized that Ross was right that she was living life always for tomorrow and never for today. How do you think they will handle life in their future?

14. Ross thought if he loved Sugar, he had to let her go to achieve her dream—but then he decided differently, and spoke up. Do you think he shouldn't have? Was he right in putting his feelings on the table? His choice would require some compromise on both parts. What do you think about that?

REQUEST YOUR FREE BOOKS!

2 FREE INSPIRATIONAL NOVELS
PLUS 2
FREE
MYSTERY GIFTS

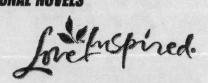

YES! Please send me 2 FREE Love Inspired® novels and my 2 FREE mystery gifts (gifts are worth about $10). After receiving them, if I don't wish to receive any more books, I can return the shipping statement marked "cancel". If I don't cancel, I will receive 4 brand-new novels every month and be billed just $4.24 per book in the U.S. or $4.74 per book in Canada, plus 25¢ shipping and handling per book and applicable taxes, if any*. That's a savings of over 20% off the cover price! I understand that accepting the 2 free books and gifts places me under no obligation to buy anything. I can always return a shipment and cancel at any time. Even if I never buy another book, the two free books and gifts are mine to keep forever.

113 IDN ERXA   313 IDN ERWX

Name	(PLEASE PRINT)	
Address		Apt. #
City	State/Prov.	Zip/Postal Code

Signature (if under 18, a parent or guardian must sign)

Order online at www.LoveInspiredBooks.com

Or mail to Steeple Hill Reader Service:

IN U.S.A.: P.O. Box 1867, Buffalo, NY 14240-1867
IN CANADA: P.O. Box 609, Fort Erie, Ontario L2A 5X3

Not valid to current subscribers of Love Inspired books.

Want to try two free books from another series?
Call 1-800-873-8635 or visit www.morefreebooks.com

* Terms and prices subject to change without notice. N.Y. residents add applicable sales tax. Canadian residents will be charged applicable provincial taxes and GST. Offer not valid in Quebec. This offer is limited to one order per household. All orders subject to approval. Credit or debit balances in a customer's account(s) may be offset by any other outstanding balance owed by or to the customer. Please allow 4 to 6 weeks for delivery. Offer available while quantities last.

Your Privacy: Steeple Hill Books is committed to protecting your privacy. Our Privacy Policy is available online at www.SteepleHill.com or upon request from the Reader Service. From time to time we make our lists of customers available to reputable third parties who have a product or service of interest to you. If you would prefer we not share your name and address, please check here. ☐

LIREG08R

Love Inspired
HISTORICAL
INSPIRATIONAL HISTORICAL ROMANCE

Cowboy Kody Douglas is a half breed, a man of two worlds who is at home in neither. When he stumbles upon Charlotte Porter's South Dakota farmhouse and finds her abandoned, he knows he can't leave her alone. Will these two outcasts find love and comfort together in a world they once thought cold and heartless?

Look for

The Journey Home
by
LINDA FORD

*Available August 2008
wherever books are sold.*

www.SteepleHill.com

Steeple
Hill®

LIH82794

TITLES AVAILABLE NEXT MONTH

Don't miss these four stories in August

HER PERFECT MAN by Jillian Hart
The McKaslin Clan
New neighbor Chad Lawson seems too perfect. At least to
Rebecca McKaslin, who's been burned by Prince Charming
before. Yet, as Rebecca gets to know Chad, his reliable, friendly
nature challenges her resistance to relationships. Maybe God put
him in her life for a reason.

LONE STAR SECRET by Lenora Worth
Homecoming Heroes
David Ryland is about to fly his final military mission. Then
he must face up to his past. His family was a mystery until his
father confessed his parentage in a deathbed letter. A letter that
Anna Terenkov knows *all* about. If David can open his heart to
the truth, will he find room for Anna?

HIDDEN TREASURES by Kathryn Springer
All work and no play is Cade Halloway's motto. His new
project: selling his family's vacation home. Yet Cade must wait
until after his sister's wedding. And deal with photographer
Meghan McBride. But what Cade doesn't know is that love is
just one of many surprises to be discovered on the property!

BLUEGRASS HERO by Allie Pleiter
Kentucky Corners
Dust-covered cowboys are the norm at Gil Sorrent's ranch. Until
a visit to Emily Montague's bath shop has them cleaning up their
acts. Now they spend more time courting than working. Gil is
determined to give Emily a piece of his mind, but it's his heart
she's after.

LICNM0708